THE MASTER OF INCHMEIG

Ann Carrol, living in a remote village on the side of a loch, longs to get away from home and see more of life than the village has to offer. Frustrated in this wish she becomes secretary to the Master of Meig House on the island in the loch. Here she finds that her life is far from the uneventful one she had thought it might become.

Caught between her employer and her father, Ann has to face experiences and emotions she had not anticipated. How she reacts to them forms the basis of this charming story.

THE MASTER OF INCHMEIG

The Master of Inchmeig

by
Margaret Starks

DALES LARGE PRINT
Long Preston, North Yorkshire,
England.

British Library Cataloguing in Publication Data

Starks, Margaret
 The master of Inchmeig.
 I. Title
 823.914 [F]

 ISBN 1–85389–234–3

First Published in Great Britain by Robert Hale Ltd., 1967.

Printed and bound in Great Britain by
Redwood Press Limited, Melksham, Wiltshire

Chapter One

THE sun was going down behind the hills and the island was beginning to darken. It was difficult now to discern the chimneys of the old house which sheltered among the trees. My father and my young sister, Jenny, would soon be coming back across the loch and it was time for me to start the evening meal. But I stayed for a moment longer at the window looking at the island. On Monday I would be crossing to it with the others; it would become a part of my life too, as it was of theirs. I could not rid myself of the feeling that it had trapped me, keeping me here in the village when, for the second time in my life, I had planned to leave.

Our village huddled on the shore of the loch beneath the lofty peaks of the hills behind. It was little more than a cluster of houses around the church, the school and a few shops. On the far side of the loch the hills went on almost to the sea and in the middle of the loch, across from the village,

7

was the island of Inchmeig.

Inchmeig had belonged to the Reddie family for as far back as anyone could remember and generations of them had lived there in Meig House, the house among the trees, known to us in the village simply as "The House". The life of the village was bound up with that of the island and the master of Meig House was virtually master of the village too for apart from the shopkeepers and one or two others such as the doctor, the minister and the school-teacher most of the villagers were employed on the island in one capacity or another.

Now the House had a new master, an Englishman and a stranger, for the old master, Duncan Reddie, had recently died and his son-in-law, Mark Sutherby, who, so far as I knew had never been near the island, had come to take his place.

My father was not happy at the change. He had worked for Duncan Reddie for most of his life and both respected and admired him. Although he didn't say so I sensed that he hadn't taken to his new master.

Until his death Duncan Reddie was a familiar figure to me as to everyone else in the village for he came across to worship in the church every Sunday. He always read the Lesson, standing large and impressive before us, and his strong voice filled the small church. Now and again he would pause to let the words sink in and then he would look up to fix some member of the congregation with his unsmiling eyes. As a child I remember searching for the comfort of my mother's hand as he left his pew, praying that his glance would not fall on me for there seemed very little difference between him and God Himself. Even as I grew up he still seemed stern and unapproachable to me. There was an arrogance about him too, in the way he carried himself and the way he accepted the humility of the villagers. My father disagreed with me when I said as much one Sunday on our way home from church.

"I'll admit he's a grandness about him, and rightly so. He's something to be proud of, you'll not deny."

"Even so, there's a hardness about him, a sort of bitterness too in the way his mouth droops at the corners."

"Nonsense. Your head's full of foolish fancies. Though he's had cause enough to feel bitterness, he not getting the son he was so set on getting to follow after him. And then the way young Fiona left him to marry

9

that Englishman right after her mother's death."

"I wonder he didn't marry again. It's years since his wife died."

"It's not so easy, lass, when you've married the right woman the first time."

I looked at him with sympathy for I guessed he was thinking of my mother, for we both knew then that she hadn't much longer to live.

"I suppose that's why he's so fond of Peter," I said after a moment, "since he didn't have a son."

"Aye. Young Peter's been more like a son than a grandson to him."

I thought of the boy as we walked on in silence. He was about the same age as my young sister and almost as familiar to us as his grandfather for he had been coming to the island for his holidays from school ever since I could remember and always came across to the church with his grandfather while he was there. He seemed a friendly and likeable lad and I suspected would often have liked to linger with some of the village boys if he'd been alone.

I couldn't remember his mother, Fiona, Duncan Reddie's only child, for she'd never been back to the island since her marriage.

10

Nor could I remember Fiona's mother, for she had died when I was a child. I had a vague recollection of standing by the jetty one day with my mother and watching the boat come across from the island bearing her coffin for the service in the church and then taking it back to the island for burial.

When Duncan Reddie died almost the whole village attended the funeral service in the church. I was among the few who did not go, for my mother too was dying and I stayed with her while my father and Jenny went to pay their respects to their late employer. The village talked of nothing but his death and the funeral and what would now happen over in the House. But there was no place for such gossip in our house, for our own private sorrow filled our thoughts.

Fiona came back for a brief visit to her old home, bringing Peter with her, and they both attended the funeral, but Fiona's husband, Mark Sutherby, was not with them. Now, after they had gone, he had come to live in the House alone.

It was a gloomy old house to live in alone, more like a fortress than a house, for it had stood on the island for well over two hundred years. It had been repaired and refurnished through the years and the land around it had been cleared and gardens laid out. It was in the gardens that my father worked, going there as a boy following in his father's footsteps, with no thought of doing anything else. That was the way it was in the village where things changed very little.

I had been across to the island as a child with my mother and remember peeping into some of the rooms of the House with the housekeeper. I suppose the family must have been away at the time. To me the House looked huge and sombre and I was awed by the size of the rooms and the height of the ceilings. My mother, I remember, was much impressed by the furnishings, especially the long, rich curtains. Later, while she was taking a cup of tea with the housekeeper, I wandered outside and since nobody was there to stop me went through the gates and beyond the gardens. On a rocky headland I found myself in the burial ground. It was just like the churchyard with its grassy mounds and old tombstones. Over to one side were some ruins which I had not known were there although I had known about the burial ground. The ruins, I discovered later, were of some ancient chapel. I could hear the waters of the loch lapping at the rocks below and the tall trees rustled high above my head. Daffodils blew wild in every corner and I thought it a secret and attractive place.

As a child the island seemed a remote place to me, far off in the middle of the loch, and I thought it very adventurous of my father to cross to it each day. Sometimes the loch was sunlit and smooth but often it was whipped into fury by the strong winds that blew down through the hills as if through a funnel. Then the boat rocked and danced as it nosed its way through the water, the waves showering it with spray as they broke around it. On such days, when the wind howled in the chimney, my mother was silent as she went about the kitchen preparing the breakfast. She would stare through the window, frowning at the lashing rain while my father put on his coat and sometimes she gave voice to her fears.

"The loch is evil. It will be a bad crossing today."

Then I was suddenly afraid for my father's safety. I had heard of people drowning in the loch. Supposing my father were to drown. But he would laugh at her fears and then I knew everything would be all right. My father was big and strong. Nothing could harm him, not even the wild waters of the loch. I never doubted the reassurance of his answer. My father always knew best, as my mother so often told me.

It was not until I was older and had left the village school to attend the distant town school that I began secretly to disagree with some of my father's ideas. Times were changing but he would never change. Nor was he alone in that, for our small, isolated community was not very much in touch with the outside world. Yet although my father was a strict disciplinarian he was not an unkindly man and we were a happy family. My mother had a gentle nature and never resisted my father's domination. In fact she had been brought up to accept it as right and proper. Although our life was simple and there was never any money to spare we were no different from most of the other people in the village and we did not miss what we had never had.

Going into the town for school soon roused in me a desire to see more of the world that lay beyond our village but guessing that these ideas would be disapproved of at home I kept my thoughts to myself. In my last years at school I took a secretarial course, hoping secretly that this would lead to a job in the town. My father at first opposed the idea of this course.

"There's a lot she's learned already she'll never use," he grumbled. "She's old enough now to be doing something useful."

"Something useful" to my father's way of thinking was something domestic, preferably over at the House.

Unexpectedly my mother sided with me.

"Ann's a bright girl. Miss Phipps at the school always said so. There'll likely be something for her at the House with this training. And if she's not to marry she'd best be doing something she likes."

"Who says she's not to marry?" my father demanded.

"I'm not saying she won't. But not every lass does."

I've wondered since if my mother had not already recognized in me an independence which she thought would prevent me finding happiness in marriage.

In the end my father consented to the secretarial course for me although I am sure that he would not have done so if he had guessed at my intentions. However, before the course was completed my mother had become an invalid and we knew she would never be well again. All ideas of a business career were forgotten, for it never occurred to anyone, not even to me, that there was any alternative but for me to stay at home to keep house and look after my mother. My sister Jenny, being eight years younger than me, was still a child.

Now, after long years of illness, my mother had died and there was nothing to keep me at home any longer. Jenny was grown up and like my father now earned her living over on the island. She had idled her way through school, showing no enthusiasm to learn anything, and had left as soon as she had been allowed to. She was quite content to work under the housekeeper at the House and was getting on very well there. My father had been responsible for getting her the job and he was pleased to receive good reports of her.

"You're doing fine. You'll be making a good wife at any rate when the time comes to wed," he told her.

Jenny blushed and giggled at this. To me she seemed a child still, probably, I suppose, because of the difference in years between us.

More than ever now since my years at home I wanted to leave the village, yet the thought of my father held me back. Jenny, I felt, would get on very well without me. But during my mother's illness my father and I had grown more close together and now that she was gone he seemed to turn to me more and more. I knew that he would take any suggestion of my leaving home as a rejection of himself and that I could not go without a bitter quarrel. Knowing him as I did, I felt that it might estrange us for good. I think that I would have faced this if my mother had been alive and well, but now I shrank from doing it, especially so soon after my mother's death. I wondered if I could break away gradually. If I got a job now I could travel to and from the town daily, at least until the winter. It would mean leaving home very early and getting back late but it was possible. Then later on, as the weather got bad and the journey more difficult, I could use that as an excuse for coming home at the weekends only. I decided to broach the subject to my father.

I waited until after supper when he was seated in his armchair in the living room. This half hour on working days after his supper was the only relaxation he allowed himself, for he could never stand idleness either in himself or others.

"Father, I'd be better taking a job now."

"Aye, lass, I've been thinking the same."

"There'll be nothing in the village for me. I'd like to do what I was trained for. I'll need to go into town."

He looked at me sharply. "You'd not manage the journey."

"I managed it for school."

"Aye, but the school bus picked you up and brought you back. You'll not get that service now."

"No, I know it'll be more difficult. But I'd like to try it and see how I get on."

He made no answer.

"I'll get everything straight here tomorrow and spend the day in town on Friday and see what I can find."

Still he made no answer and I held my peace. I had made the first move.

When he returned from the island the following day I could tell by his manner that he had something on his mind. However, he said nothing until we had finished our meal. Jenny had taken the dishes into the kitchen to wash them and I was just about to follow her when he stopped me.

"There's work for you at the House," he said bluntly. "The kind that you want."

I looked at him in surprise.

"I've spoken to Mr Sutherby. He could do with a secretary it seems and he's willing to give you a try."

This was a turn of events I hadn't expected.

"I may not suit Mr Sutherby," I said. "After all, I've had no experience yet."

"You've had no experience for the town either," he said sharply, and after a moment added, "He wants you from Monday to Friday. You'll have Saturdays to yourself for the shopping and the house. You won't get anything else as convenient as that."

I stood looking at him, not knowing quite what to say.

"You'd best think it over, lass. I've to take him your answer tomorrow."

I thought it over for the rest of the evening, but at the back of my mind I knew I was caught. I told myself that it need be only for a short time. Time for my father to get over the death of my mother. Time in which after all I might get the experience I lacked.

So I had decided to go and now as I looked across at the island black against the sunset I wondered if my decision had been the right one. I was already twenty-five and time seemed to be slipping away fast.

Perhaps soon I should feel that I was already too old to break away, to start out on my own. My father's life was bound up with the island. Jenny seemed content for hers to be too. Was I going to follow suit?

I drew the curtains against the gathering darkness and turned from the window, trying to push my doubts aside by busying myself with the preparations for supper.

As I spread the tablecloth on the small round table in the living room, where we took all our meals, and put around the knives and forks I wondered what kind of work I would be expected to do and what the man I would be working for was like. There had been plenty of gossip about him in the village and I was sorry now that I had paid so little heed to it.

"What's Mr Sutherby like?" I asked my father later, when we were seated at the supper table.

"He's right enough. You'll do fine," he said shortly, obviously not intending to expand on this.

"I wonder when Fiona's coming back."

"I don't believe she's coming back at all," Jenny said quickly, looking up from her plate with a sparkle of excitement in her eyes. "Do you think they're divorced or something?"

My father's frown put a stop to any speculation on this subject.

"Such blethering! Don't you be letting your curiosity concern you in what is no business of yours."

But later on, in the little bedroom which we shared, Jenny said in a whisper so that my father would not overhear in the next room:

"I don't care what father says, I don't believe Mrs Sutherby is coming back. That's what they're saying at the House anyway. Peter's coming here for his holidays though just the same, so Mrs Willis says."

My curiosity too was now aroused. It was strange that Fiona had come to her father's funeral without her husband and that now he was living at the House she was not there. But I shrugged these thoughts aside. I was not very concerned with them. All that really mattered to me was what kind of person Mr Sutherby would prove to be and whether I should like working for him. And that I shall find out quickly enough, I thought as I climbed into bed.

Chapter Two

A THIN mist hung over the loch as we made our way through the village to the jetty on the Monday morning. I was surprised to find myself feeling rather nervous and I envied Jenny her lightheartedness. I answered her chatter briefly, lost in my own thoughts, as we followed my father's striding figure down the narrow path.

The boat which was to take us across to the island was tied up alongside the jetty. It was a fair-sized dinghy with an outboard motor and I noticed that it was newly painted in dark green with the name *Singing Wren* in bold white letters across the prow. It belonged to Andrew Mellor, the owner of the only shop of any size in the village, who had an arrangement of many years standing to ferry the villagers who worked on the island across and back. In addition to his passengers, he usually carried supplies of groceries for the House. He had ferried the workers himself for as long as I could remember and I was surprised now to see his eldest son, Tom, waiting by the boat.

"Where's Mr Mellor this morning?" I asked Jenny as we came up to the jetty. "Is he ill, do you know?"

"No, he's all right," she answered lightly. "Tom's been ferrying for a while now, didn't you know?"

"The boat's looking very smart," I said. "I thought it was a new one at first. It's changed its name too. It was never called that."

She gave me a quick look and laughed. "That's Tom's doing."

Most of the people were already seated in the boat, for with the three of us going off we had left a little later than my father and Jenny usually did. I had been used to clearing the breakfast away after they had gone but this morning we had hastily done it together. Tom helped us into the boat and Jenny went and sat in the stern. Rob Davie, a young man of much the same age as myself, sat on a side seat next to Meg, the girl who worked with Jenny, and he gave her a playful push.

"Move over, Meg. We've another lady aboard this morning."

He patted the seat beside him and I sat down rather reluctantly. I had no liking for Rob who had once or twice tried to force his attentions on me.

The last straggler arrived and Tom started the boat. The sun showed faintly through the mist above the hills on the near shore and as we turned about I looked towards the island but it was still shrouded in mist. My father, who was sitting near me, noticed my glance and for a moment he rested his hand on mine. In the morning light his craggy face looked full of hollows and his once dark hair was streaked with grey. He was beginning to show his years; I had noticed the stoop of his shoulders as we walked behind him. I was glad now that I had stayed with him.

Rob made one or two attempts to draw me into conversation but I was not feeling talkative and after a while he gave up and turned to Meg. Tom had seated himself beside Jenny and was talking to her as he steered the boat through the still water. I was struck by the way they were looking at each other and I studied him with a new interest. He was an open-faced, cheerful boy with rather mischievous eyes. I'd known him from a child of course but had not noticed before how he had grown up. He was now a young man, about two years older than Jenny, and not at all bad looking. In fact his quick, easy movements and his swarthy skin gave him rather a dashing appearance. He and Jenny, it seemed to me, were obviously more than a little interested in each other, although Jenny had never spoken about him to me.

I looked at Jenny with new eyes. Her chestnut curls were carefully arranged and she had tied a flimsy scarf over her hair to keep it in place. Her brown eyes rested on Tom's face as she leaned forward slightly, talking to him. Lately she had taken to spending a long time in front of the mirror, trying out different ways of doing her hair, and she had become very conscious of her clothes. I had been amused and a little irritated, thinking her empty headed. Now I wondered if she was quite such a baby as I supposed.

The sun had at last broken through and the mist was rapidly retreating to the far side of the loch. We were approaching the island and now it showed clear in the sunlight. I could see the house among the trees, the smoke rising from its chimneys. As we came abreast the main jetty, where the boats belonging to the House were moored, I could see the gravel drive leading up to the front entrance.

The *Singing Wren* landed at a smaller jetty farther along the shore and from here a rough track led up through the edge of the woods to the rear of the house. Tom leaped on to the jetty with the nimbleness I'd noted and tied up the boat then gave us a hand to help us ashore. The men immediately set off through the woods, leaving the three of us behind with Tom. Jenny lingered with him as he began to unload the groceries and Meg put her arm through mine.

"Come away," she said with a laugh, giving me a teasing pull. "Jenny can catch us up."

She caught up with us just as we reached the house.

"You'd better find Mrs Willis," she said to me. "Come on. I'll take you to her room."

We went through the kitchen and along a rather gloomy passage to the housekeeper's room and Jenny knocked on the door. Mrs Willis answered from inside and Jenny grinned at me.

"In you go." She turned and sped back down the passage and I opened the door and went in.

The room was rather dark with one tall narrow window, but I had a brief impression of cosiness nevertheless, perhaps because of the bright fire that burned in the grate. Mrs Willis had known my mother and she gave me a friendly welcome.

"I hope you'll be happy here. It's nice to be with your father and Jenny."

Her friendliness helped to dispel my nervousness. "I hope I'll be able to do the work. After all, it's my first job."

"I don't think you'll find Mr Sutherby difficult to work for, though he's a strange man in some ways. You'll not be seeing him this morning for he's away on the estate somewhere, but he's left some work for you to get on with. Come, I'll show you the little office we've fitted out for you."

I followed her towards the front of the house and into the large entrance hall. The heavy outer doors were open and the inner glass door let in a stream of sunlight. I remembered standing there as a child holding my mother's hand. The front door on the right must lead into the great drawing room and that on the left into the dining room. Mrs Willis smiled as she watched me looking around.

"Do you remember the day you came across with your mother? You were only a wee thing then. It must have been many years ago."

She pointed out the door behind the dining room. "That's Mr Sutherby's office and yours is this room behind it."

She led me to the door at the back of the hall and I followed her inside. It was a small high-ceilinged room with one narrow window, rather like a cell in its bareness, for the walls were distempered in white and completely unadorned. But the whiteness gave an effect of light to the room and in the small fireplace a cheerful fire burned. A table stood over by the window with a typewriter and a pile of papers on it and through the window was an attractive view of the side garden. A coat rack and small mirror were fastened to the wall beside the door and the only other piece of furniture was a small armchair drawn up beside the fireplace. The floor was of varnished wood and in front of the fireplace was a tufted rug, that and the armchair being the only gesture to comfort or luxury. Yet I was pleased with my little office and Mrs Willis must have read the approval on my face, for she smiled.

"It's hardly a grand room, in fact it's been used as a store room for years. But at least it has a fireplace. And a chimney that doesn't smoke too," she added, "which is more than can be said for some of the larger rooms in the house. It's the best room we could give you because there's a connecting door with Mr Sutherby's study."

She went to the second door, which was in the wall opposite the fireplace, and opened it.

"You might as well take a look in his room since he's not here."

This was a grand room of fine proportion with bookshelves from floor to ceiling filled with rows of leatherbound books. It had three long windows with leaded panes and window seats and a large, impressive fireplace with gleaming copper firearms. The floor was carpeted and there were several deep, leather armchairs around the room and a long settee beside the fireplace. A huge mahogany desk littered with papers with a swivel chair beside it completed the furnishings.

"Well, I'll show you the work Mr Sutherby has left for you and then I must leave you," Mrs Willis said briskly as she closed the door again.

There was a pile of closely written pages on the desk with instructions as to how they were to be typed.

"It's the manuscript of the book he's writing," Mrs Willis explained. "He's what they call a historian."

The writing seemed reasonably legible and I felt that at least the morning's work was not going to be beyond me. As soon as Mrs Willis left me I began to work.

Jenny came in half-way through the morning with a tray.

"Tea," she said cheerfully as she came around the door. "Mrs Willis thought you might like me to bring mine in with you this morning since you are alone."

She perched herself on a corner of the desk. "So you haven't met Mr Sutherby yet?"

I shook my head as I sipped the tea.

"I wonder how you'll get on with him," she said with a note of curiosity in her voice.

"Not so well as you seem to with Tom Mellor."

She gave a little laugh. "I knew it wouldn't take long for you to find out. Father doesn't seem to have noticed yet."

"Tom's a nice boy," I said.

"Do you think so?"

I laughed at her eagerness. "Does it matter what I think?"

"Yes, it does. I'd like you on my side if Father starts objecting."

"Is it that serious?" I asked with amusement.

"Yes, it is," she said rather crossly. "Though I can't see Father thinking so. He thinks I'm still a child."

I stopped myself in time from saying "Well, aren't you?" for I had no wish to quarrel with her. I watched her as she sat there swinging her legs, a small frown of concentration on her face. Suddenly she turned to me, her face eager again.

"What do you think of the boat?"

"The boat?"

"Yes. The name Tom's given it."

For a moment I had difficulty in remembering it.

"Don't you see? It's named after me."

Jenny Carroll. The *Singing Wren*. I threw back my head and laughed. "I had no idea Tom was so poetic."

She jumped down from the desk. "I think it's a very nice idea," she said, tossing her head, her eyes sparking in anger.

As I continued to laugh she collected up the cups and made for the door. "You're as bad as Father," she stopped to say when she had opened it. "You never take anything I do seriously." She pulled the door angrily behind her with her foot and I was sorry that I had upset her.

I returned to my work again and became

31

so interested in what I was copying that I did not notice how swiftly the time passed. I was surprised when Jenny stuck her head around the door.

"You must like your work. Don't you know it's lunch time?" She had recovered her good humour and we went along the passage together.

Meg and Jenny ate their lunch in the kitchen, but Mrs Willis invited me to have mine with her in her room. It seemed strange at first sitting in there, knowing Jenny was in the kitchen, but Mrs Willis chatted away to me and I soon forgot about it. After lunch Mrs Willis liked to sit back in an armchair and close her eyes for a short rest and I went out to find the other two. They had taken a couple of chairs outside the kitchen door and were sitting there in the sunshine. I felt too restless to sit down with them and after a moment decided to go for a walk.

I went down the path through the woods and wandered along the strip of stony beach, walking away from the house. The beach ended by a rocky headland and I found myself outside the burial ground that I had discovered as a child. It was separated from the rest of the island by a low wall but the gates stood wide open as they had apparently been for years. A steeply sloping path led down to the water. Impelled by curiosity, I walked up the path and through the gates. It was as I remembered it. I could hear the water lapping on the rocks below and the tall trees were still high above my head. The daffodils were there too but not yet in flower. Most of the headstones were so old that I could no longer read the inscriptions but on one side of the ground was a row of relatively new ones belonging to the Reddie family. Newest of all was that of Duncan Reddie and I stood by his grave for a moment remembering what I knew of him.

A voice behind me jerked me out of my daydream with its startling unexpectedness, for I had thought I was alone.

"Worshipping at the great man's shrine, I see."

I turned swiftly to face a man whom I knew at once must be Mr Sutherby. I had not heard him approach on the springy turf. He stood there, hands in pockets, scrutinizing me from beneath shaggy eyebrows drawn down into a frown. His face was unsmiling and his voice had an acid edge to it. I thought that I had been missing for longer than I realized and that he had been looking for me.

"I'm sorry," I said. "I'm afraid I didn't realise how the time had gone."

"Time," he said with a slight shrug. "Who worries about time in this place? It seems to have stood still. Things haven't changed much here since the wild tribesmen chased each other through the hills."

He nodded his head towards the graves of the Reddie family. "I don't believe these upstarts were any more civilized than the earlier masters of this island. Not if the last was anyone to go by, anyway. You look shocked. I speak irreverently of your dead hero."

I disliked the sarcasm in his voice and I answered rather stiffly. "I scarcely knew him. But I have a reverence for the dead."

He gave a short laugh which was not pleasant to hear. "And I suppose you see him now as a chubby little cherub, floating somewhere above the clouds."

I made no answer to this and I wished that I could go back to the house. But he stood there blocking my way and he made no move to go. He stayed there silent, staring ahead of him, seeming now to ignore my existence and as I was turned towards

34

him I observed him more attentively. He was of medium height with thick, sandy-coloured hair which he wore rather long and brushed back from his forehead so that it curled somewhat boyishly around his ears. I thought that he was around forty. He was neatly dressed, in fact he appeared almost dandified by comparison with what I was used to seeing. Such a suit as he wore could certainly not be purchased in the village nor would it be asked for.

He turned suddenly to find me staring at him and I felt the colour come to my cheeks before his own cool gaze.

"So you've followed your father and sister. What attracts you villagers to this God-forsaken place?"

His manner made politeness difficult.

"There's no attraction for me here. I came only to please my father."

"Ah. You mean you don't want to work for me. No doubt you've been listening to the gossip and rumours that run around here like rats in a barn."

"I was not influenced by gossip. I didn't want to come to the island."

He looked at me curiously for a moment. "Well, that makes two of us. At least we have one thing in common."

He continued looking at me and I began to find this habit of his quite disconcerting.

"So you came because that's what your father wanted. Of course, I'd forgotten. Women are still in bondage in these parts. When they escape their fathers it's only to be enslaved by their husbands. Have you not the spirit to break away?"

"I have every intention of doing so," I said with some heat, angered by the almost contemptuous way he spoke. "I'll not stay long on the island."

He raised his eyebrows at this and said quietly, "Indeed. Well, shall we go back and find out if you're to have the opportunity of staying on the island at all?"

He walked away and I followed him unhappily, aware that I had made a bad start.

As we came up to the house I took the path that led to the back entrance, thinking to go in the way I had come out, but he called me back.

"Where are you off to now?" he said testily.

I stopped and looked at him. "Into the house." As you know very well, I thought.

"Don't you think it would be more companionable to go in together since we're to work together? I doubt if my presence in the kitchen would be appreciated, so I suggest we use the front entrance. Don't be afraid," he added as I hesitated, "there's no big ogre now to scare you off." I knew he was referring to Duncan Reddie, for in his time nobody but guests to the house would have presumed to use the front entrance.

I followed him into the hall and he held the door of his room open for me to pass through.

"There are some letters I want to deal with first."

By now I was feeling very nervous, for I thought such an irascible man was going to be hard to please. But I had no difficulty in taking down the letters at his dictation. I would have had time to take them down in longhand. When he had finished he sat back in his chair with his hands folded behind his head and watched me while I gathered up my things.

"What do you think of this room?"

He shot the question at me suddenly and for a moment I was too surprised to answer.

"Well, I asked you a question."

"I think it's very grand," I said, glancing around it.

"Do you. Well I think it's very gloomy

and depressing. It's heavy and pretentious. Far too much like its late occupant," he added, frowning at me accusingly as if I were responsible.

His slighting references to his dead father-in-law seemed to me in very poor taste.

"Is that such a bad thing?" I couldn't resist asking.

"I think it is. But I can see you're like the rest of them. Off you go and get those letters done."

I accepted the abrupt dismissal and went into my own room. Some time later the door opened and he stood there in the doorway looking about him, first I thought, in astonishment and then in amusement. Finally he burst into laughter. I had no idea what was amusing him and I sat watching him, waiting for him to speak. Now that the sour lines were lifted from his face he looked much younger and I noticed that his eyes, which were usually half-hidden under his frowning brows, were rather fine. They were a golden brown with lighter flecks in them. I thought that if he were more human he would be quite attractive.

"Well, I can see why you think my room so magnificent," he said at last. "I remember now. This place was stacked with old books and lumber when I looked in here before. Well, well," he added, coming farther into the room. "The great man himself couldn't have objected to your being housed in here."

He looked around the bare walls. "It's as austere as a convent. But it suits you," he said, turning to me. "Oh yes. I can well imagine those grey eyes of yours, which appraise me so coolly, looking out through a wimple."

Then his manner changed and he said brusquely:

"I came to change one of the letters but I see you've finished them. Well, it's not that important. Leave it as it is."

He picked up the pages of the manuscript I had typed that morning and inspected them. "You can carry on with this now," he said.

He took the letters and went to the door. "For my part, you can stay on the island as long as you wish. But I shall expect some notice remember, if and when you find the courage to spread your wings."

I saw no more of him for the rest of the afternoon. When I put my head round the door, thinking it only polite to tell him I was going, he was standing with his hands in his pockets staring up at the bookshelves and he gave no sign that he had heard me. I closed the door quietly and went in search of the others.

Jenny had already gone down to the boat, but Meg was waiting for me.

"Jenny's away as soon as she can," she said with a laugh. "Tom gets over a bit early. We'd better hurry up and get down there before the men, or your father'll start asking why Jenny's away when I'm not."

I was rather amused at the way Jenny seemed to have Meg in her pocket, for she was nearer my age than Jenny's and had worked at the House much longer. She was a heavily built girl and rather plain and it was clear that she thought Jenny attractive and was good-natured enough to feel no jealousy.

Tom and Jenny were sitting close together on the edge of the jetty when we arrived and when he saw us Tom stood up. He gave me a somewhat cheeky grin and asked me how I'd enjoyed my first day. I wondered if Jenny had told him that I had laughed at the name of his boat. They sat next to each other going back across the loch and I noticed that everybody took the seat they had occupied that morning. If this were the practice it would account in part for my father not noticing the growing friendship between Tom and Jenny.

My father said very little on the journey home, but later in the evening he questioned me about my day.

"Well, lass. Do you think you're going to suit the job?"

"Oh, I think so, Father. The work's not too difficult. Most of the time I'm just typing out a manuscript. Mr Sutherby's writing a book."

My father gave a contemptuous little snort. "He's a deal too soft and bookish. There's little he can do without being led by the hand. If you ask me it's John Martin who's running the estate now no matter who gives the orders. But don't you be forgetting who's the boss," he added sternly, as if it were I who was complaining. "There's a good job there for you if you behave yourself."

I didn't say so to my father, but I couldn't help wondering how long I would be able to "behave myself," as he put it, working for so testy and difficult a man. However, it seemed most unlikely that I was going to be bored at any rate and I found myself looking forward to going back to the island in the morning.

Chapter Three

IF the life of the village and the island changed very little, one thing that varied constantly was the weather. Within an hour the loch and the whole wild countryside around could change completely. A tempestuous wind that boiled the loch, raced the rainclouds and darkened the hills could die almost on the instant, calming the loch and leaving the skies clear and the hills a kaleidoscope of colour. A beautiful sunset that promised a fair tomorrow would most likely be followed by a stormy dawn.

As we stood on the jetty the next morning waiting to board the boat the calm of the previous day had vanished and a gusty wind raised the waters of the loch to white-foamed peaks and tore at our clothes. We were all used to the vagaries of the weather, but we were glad nevertheless to huddle down in the boat as it headed through the turbulent water. Rob Davie opened his coat with a playful gesture of gallantry, offering to share it with Meg and me. Meg accepted his offer laughingly, but I shook my head, trying not to look too unfriendly. Jenny had her coat collar up and her stray curls were blowing in the wind. Her cheeks were rosy and her eyes bright. Meg's right, I thought, she's really bonny. If my hair blows like that I just look untidy. She caught me looking at her and gave me a cheeky wink as Tom sat down beside her. I had to smile and I looked at my father to see if he had noticed, but he was turned away, talking to one of the men.

I was feeling more relaxed this morning, even to the point of making myself agreeable to Rob. But after a while I fell silent and as we neared the island he turned and looked at me and then said to the others, "See how quiet Ann is, now we're near the House. She's feeling the gloom of the Englishman already."

They all laughed and it seemed to me that it wasn't just my father who'd taken a dislike to the new master of the island.

"Away with you and your jokes, Rob," my father said. "The lass is doing fine."

But Rob hadn't been so far from the truth, for I had been thinking of Mr

Sutherby and wondering what sort of mood I should find him in.

When I reached my room I saw that no new work had been put on my desk. I wondered if I should carry on with the manuscript, but decided that I'd better find out first if Mr Sutherby was in his room in case there was something else he wanted me to do.

I tapped on his door and hearing no reply opened it and looked in. He was there, seated at his desk, with a bulky scarf around his neck. He looked up with his characteristic scowl as I said good-morning to him.

"So you're not drowned, nor even seasick. You must be tougher than you look to be so cheerful after crossing in this weather."

A gust of wind shook the windows and a cloud of smoke blew down the chimney. He huddled deeper in his chair and pulled the scarf higher round his ears.

"Only the tough could survive here, anyway," he grumbled. "I can sit by the fire and choke or sit by the window and have my head blown off in order to breathe."

He stood up, pushing his chair back with an irritable gesture, and began walking up and down, chafing his hands to warm them.

He looked an amusing figure in his neat suit, muffled as he was in the heavy scarf, and his scowling face reminded me of a disagreeable child.

"You can smile. You're obviously as impervious to discomfort as everyone else in this vast sieve."

"Shall I carry on with the manuscript or is there something else you want me to do?" I asked.

He ignored my question. "Does the spring ever come to this outlandish place?"

"We have our days," I said quietly.

"Oh, go and shut yourself in your cell, and get on with the manuscript," he said rudely, turning his back on me.

I saw no more of him during the morning although I heard considerable movement in his room and knew that he was still there.

At lunch time Mrs Willis asked me how I was getting on. "Do you think you're going to like working for Mr Sutherby?"

I answered rather evasively. "Oh yes. So far I've found the work quite easy."

She looked at me a little curiously. "He's not the easiest of people to get on with, I know. He might be a little less crotchety now his belongings have arrived though. He's been very impatient for them.

45

"His books and music and things," she explained, seeing my look of enquiry. "They came over this morning. Perhaps he'll settle down better now."

After lunch I left her beside the fire and decided to go for a walk. The wind was much less boisterous but still chilly and I set out briskly across the island. The island is long but quite narrow in places and I knew that if I walked fast I would have time to walk across to the other shore and back.

I went through the woods and across some open grassland, jumping the small streamlets and climbing over the many loose-stoned low walls that criss-cross the island. Presently I came out to the farther shore and, hot now from my scramble, sat down on a large boulder to rest for a few moments before going back. The wind blew cool on my face and I leaned back on my hands watching the hills change colour as the clouds blew over them.

I heard a step close beside me and turning my head quickly I saw Mr Sutherby coming towards me.

"Oh sit down, do," he said testily and somewhat breathlessly as I got to my feet. "I've followed you far enough."

"You followed me?" I said in

astonishment as I sat down rather more slowly than I had got up.

"Yes. I saw you leave the house and I thought I was going to have a walking companion. But you hared off at such a rate that I couldn't catch up with you. Do you always move at such a speed?"

Remembering the scramble I had had, I was amused at the idea of him following me and I smiled.

"I wanted to see this side of the island and I knew there wasn't much time. I ought to be getting back now."

"Well, since it's for my benefit, I assume, that you're hurrying back, you can stifle that conscience of yours for once, also for my benefit, so that we can return a trifle more leisurely than we came."

He stood beside me looking across the loch, making no move to go. "You seem to me to belong here. Why are you so anxious to escape?"

"I want to see something of the world before I'm too old."

"You have a little time yet," he said drily. I felt his eyes on me. "You're not much like your sister."

"Jenny takes after my mother," I said, and remembering her face as she looked that morning I added, "She's growing to be quite pretty, too."

"I didn't mean in looks," he said. "You have your father's independence. Or perhaps I should say stubbornness."

I kept a rather resentful silence. Had he followed me just to analyse my character? And in no complimentary way at that.

"Let us go back," he said at last. "But not by your madcap route. There is an easier way, more suited to my years, to say nothing of my exalted position as Lord of the Island."

There was no smile on his face and no hint of humour in his eyes as he regarded me, yet I sensed a little more friendliness in his attitude towards me. Mrs Willis was right, I thought, as we started back, he is in a better humour than he was this morning.

He hardly spoke on the way back and I made no attempt at conversation either, for he seemed to me the most difficult person to talk to. When we reached the house he invited me into the study and I thought that he had some more letters to dictate. As I entered the room I noticed at once that he had been making changes in it. The large portrait of Duncan Reddie that had hung above the mantelpiece was gone and in its place was a painting of a rural scene with a small church, a farm and a cluster of cottages. All the other pictures had been changed too and the ornaments and knick-knacks that had stood around before had been removed and others put in their place. Most noticeable of all, one whole wall had been stripped of the heavy, uniform volumes and filled with books in modern bindings. Books of all colours and sizes now filled the shelves.

He stood watching me as I looked about me at the changes. "Well," he said impatiently, "don't you think these things a great improvement on the old?"

"They're very attractive," I said, "but . . ."

"But what? What's your objection?"

"It's just that they don't really belong here."

His face went hard and I saw anger in his eyes. "Just as I don't belong here. That's what you mean, isn't it?"

He stalked off and sat down at his desk, pulling his papers towards him and ignoring me. I watched him for a moment, a little nettled myself at his touchiness, for I had meant nothing of the sort. Then I walked across to his desk and said quietly:

"If you fitted into this room – into this house – as you seem to want to – in fact if you filled Duncan Reddie's place so exactly that nobody noticed the difference, wouldn't it mean that you were a good bit like him? I haven't noticed any great admiration for him on your part."

He looked up swiftly and for a moment his face was a study of varying emotions. In the end he actually smiled and again I thought how attractive his face was then.

"Well, whether you think the room incongruous now or not makes little difference. It stays as it is. I couldn't stand it for long as it was.

"There's one thing I'll thank old Duncan for," he went on, getting up from his desk, "and that's for getting the house wired as he did. I can use my music box and that soothes me quite a bit. No doubt you'll be pleased to know that."

He went over to the corner of the room where I now noticed that he had a gramophone.

"I like to work to music. You can leave your door open if you do too."

He saw me eyeing the stack of records. "Not a piper or a lament among them," he said, and now his eyes actually had a sparkle of mischief, "so you may prefer to close your door after all."

From then on I found him a much less difficult person to get on with. He played his records most of the time he was in the study and the connecting door between our rooms now stayed open. He was enthusiastic about his music and sometimes, when he was in a good mood, he would talk to me about it, telling me about the lives of the composers and the artists and the stories behind the many operas he played. This was all new and fascinating to me, for we had never paid much attention to music at home. Very soon I came to appreciate it as he did and the days passed swiftly and happily against such a background.

It was the same with his books too. He was widely read and intensely interesting to listen to when he was in the mood for talking, and he gave me permission to borrow from the shelves as I pleased.

Yet he was still not popular on the island nor in the village. He was a stranger to begin with, and his own personality kept him a stranger. I often wondered why he had come to live there since he disliked it so much. It was as if he had made himself a prisoner on the island, for he never left it, and to me he seemed a very lonely person.

One of the things for which he was much criticized was the fact that he didn't come across to the church on Sundays. My father was outspoken about this.

"Perhaps it's because he doesn't like our different kind of service," I suggested.

My father was contemptuous of this idea. "He doesn't like any kind of service. What happened when the minister went across to invite him to read the lesson? All he got for his trouble was to be told that our Englishman was not in the habit of attending church and was not going to start now. The man's a heathen, like most of his countrymen. The minister says the English churches are nearly empty. The lad's coming home tomorrow, so I hear. Let's hope he'll not stop him from coming to the church. He always came with his grand-father."

"I should think Mr Sutherby's looking forward to his coming. He must feel very lonely at times."

"If he's lonely he's only himself to blame," my father said shortly, dismissing the subject.

Although Peter was coming to the island, Mr Sutherby had not mentioned him. In

52

fact although he talked to me now about many different things, he never spoke about himself or his affairs and if ever the conversation seemed to be headed that way he would change the subject abruptly.

I asked Mrs Willis if Fiona would be coming with Peter.

"Mr Sutherby hasn't said so," she said. I could see that she had no wish to pursue the matter and I said no more. But I couldn't help wondering why she still hadn't come to the island. Perhaps with Peter's coming I would find out.

On the day when Peter was expected I didn't see Mr Sutherby all the morning. He was not in his study when I arrived, although I heard him come in later and then go out again without calling out a good-morning to me as he usually did if he came in after me. I didn't see him after lunch either when I set out for my walk. This had become a daily habit with me now unless the weather made it impossible and quite frequently he would join me.

Spring had at last come to the island and the buds were bursting on the trees. Daffodils bloomed in profusion and the flowering trees were in blossom in the gardens. The sun was warm and after I'd been walking for a while I sat down on a bank beside one of the streams where the primroses poked through the moss. I had not been there long when I caught sight of Mr Sutherby walking in my direction. Even from a distance I saw the gloom in his face, the old familiar scowl. He saw me sitting there and stopped, making no sign of recognition, then he turned and walked in a different direction.

I was used to his moods by now, for even though he had mellowed considerably he could still flare up suddenly or take a fit of sulks. I had found it best to take no notice and quietly leave him to recover. When we met again he would behave as if nothing had happened and never once did he apologize for his behaviour. Something, it seemed, had upset him today, and I wondered what it could be.

When I went back to my room I could hear him moving around in his. I had plenty of work to get on with and I sat down at my desk, waiting for him to come round from his ill-humour. By the end of the afternoon he had still not spoken to me and when I went to put my work on his desk and tell him I was going he was standing with his back to me, staring out of the window.

From the droop of his shoulders he looked more dejected than bad-tempered. He didn't turn round and I hesitated for a moment, then, thinking to part on a friendly note, said:

"You must be looking forward very much to this evening?"

"Must I?" he said icily without turning round. "Why?"

His manner made me feel I had said something I shouldn't and that he was waiting to see what I would say next.

"I meant because Peter's coming home," I said a little uncertainly, expecting one of his outbursts, though not understanding why.

He turned round then and stared at me sourly, yet in spite of his disagreeable expression I saw the strain in his face, as if he were more unhappy than anything else. He said nothing but stood looking at me in such a way that I began to feel I was intruding by being there. I put my work on his desk and left him.

I found myself thinking about him more than once during the evening. I could think of nothing I had said or done to put him in the mood he had been in all day. And my reference to Peter had done nothing to shake him out of it. For a moment I wondered if it were Peter's homecoming that disturbed him, but the thought seemed so unreasonable I put it from my mind. I decided I would never understand this strange man.

Chapter Four

AS we drew near the island the following morning we saw a figure bending over one of the boats belonging to the House.

"That's the lad Peter," one of the men said and he cupped his hands and shouted across the water, "Hullo there."

Peter straightened up and waved to us and Tom stood up in the boat and waved his cap.

"He'll be missing his grandfather," another man said. "He used to take the lad everywhere. His father hasn't the same interest in things."

"The boy's a Reddie, right enough. Takes after his mother," my father remarked, watching Peter. "And he's none the worse for that."

As our boat turned in to the jetty Peter came along the shore to meet it. He seemed to know most of the men and while he talked to them I had time to observe him. He was of Jenny's age and taller and more mature than I remembered him. His hair was dark and curly and his dark eyes were full of fun as he returned some of the men's banter. He appeared to be very popular with them and I could not help comparing him with his father.

When the men had gone he turned to us and from the way he and Tom greeted each other it was obvious they knew each other well. He was very polite and I thought quite charming and I noticed the quick look of interest he gave Jenny who stood smiling at him.

Meg and I started along the track and after a moment's hesitation Jenny joined us, leaving the boys together.

"He's a fine boy, right enough," said Meg, referring to Peter. "And don't you be making Tom jealous," she added teasingly to Jenny.

"Away with you, Meg," Jenny protested. "He's not for me and well you know it."

The two of them laughed and chattered on their way up to the house, but I was silent, remembering Mr Sutherby's behaviour of the day before. Surely he must be in a good mood today with Peter here. The boy was so cheerful and lively.

He was already in his room and he called me in right away to deal with the letters. I soon saw that he was still very morose. He made no attempt at conversation and the heavy silence when he was not dictating began to oppress me.

We had almost finished when there was a tap on the door and Peter came in. "Good-morning, Father," he said. "Sorry I wasn't at breakfast."

There was a restraint in his manner now that had not been there when I'd seen him earlier and his face had lost its liveliness. I wondered why he had been hanging around the jetty instead of coming in to breakfast. No doubt he was aware of his father's mood and had been avoiding him, I thought; and small wonder.

He looked around the room and I guessed it was the first time he had been in there since his return. He stood for a moment examining the shelves of new books. "I wonder what Grandfather would say if he could see his study now?" he said quietly.

He moved around the room, touching

things as if remembering. He seemed lost in his thoughts. His father was watching him closely from under his frowning brows and I suddenly realised how tense he was. There was a feeling of strain in the room, something between these two that I didn't understand, and I thought that I had better go and leave them together.

Peter spoke before I could move. "It doesn't seem the same here without grandfather. He was so much a part of this place."

To my surprise I saw his father go white, as if he'd been struck a blow, and for a moment there was a look of deep hurt in his eyes as they rested on his son. Then his face hardened again and he said with cold sarcasm, "I cannot hope to take his place here, of course, but I trust you will not find the change too unbearable."

Peter turned sharply. "Why must you always take everything I say the wrong way, Father? I wasn't comparing him with you."

His face was flushed and he looked quite distressed. "Anyway, I do miss him and I'm sorry he's dead even if you are not."

His father didn't answer and for a moment they stood looking at each other, then Peter turned away and went from the room.

I felt my own cheeks burning and I was angry with Mr Sutherby for upsetting Peter as he had, for I could see no reason for it. As if he sensed my disapproval, he pushed the letters aside and dismissed me with a curt gesture of his hand.

For a day or so after that things went on much as usual. Mr Sutherby went on with his writing as if Peter were not there, but the pleasant, friendly atmosphere in which we had lately been working was no longer there. He was silent now, shut in on himself, only talking to me about the work.

Once or twice I saw Peter out fishing on the loch and he was often at the jetty when our boat came in. For one so young and full of life he seemed a lonely figure, looking for company wherever he could get it and I couldn't understand why he couldn't get it from his father.

Mrs Willis also was troubled by the strained relationship between the two. She was not generally given to gossip, especially about the affairs of the House, but now she spoke freely about them to me.

"That boy needs company, but his father just shuts himself away. It's almost as if they deliberately avoid each other. Peter never comes in to breakfast until his father's gone and when they do take meals together you'd think they were a couple of strangers. Makes me quite uncomfortable. It doesn't seem natural."

"Yes, I've noticed it too," I said, "and I can't understand it. Mr Sutherby's always seemed lonely, too, to me, and I would have thought he'd be glad of Peter's company."

"Well, the boy was always happy enough here with his grandfather, but he seems miserable now."

I met Peter one day towards the end of the week, when I was out walking at lunch time. As I walked along the beach I saw him at the edge of the loch idly kicking pebbles into the water. He turned round quickly as he heard my approach and the rather sombre expression on his face brightened as I waved to him.

"Where are you going?" he asked, as I came up.

"Just for a walk. I usually do after lunch."

"Do you mind if I come too?"

"Of course not," I said, smiling at him. "It's nice to have company."

"It's nice for me to have cheerful company," he said as he walked beside me.

"How do you like working for my father?"

"Very much. The work is very interesting."

"I wasn't really thinking so much of the work. Don't you find him difficult to get on with?"

"Sometimes he's a bit touchy," I said cautiously. "But it's really only on the surface. He's quite different underneath."

"If you can get underneath," he said. "I've never known anyone so good at keeping his distance."

We walked in silence for a while and Peter's thoughts were obviously still on his father, for presently he said, "He's always kept me at a distance. Sent me away to school as soon as he could. Packed me off up here as soon as I came home for the holidays. Sometimes I wonder if he actually hates me."

"Oh no," I said, shocked. "I'm sure that's not true."

"Well, he hated my grandfather. I'm certain of that. Yet Grandfather was more like a father to me than he was. We've scarcely known each other, but he can't blame me for that. I thought that being up here now with him we might get to know each other better. But he doesn't really want me here. I can see that. I suppose I'm only here because my mother wants to be free of me too."

I saw the distress in his face and knew how intensely unhappy he was.

Impulsively I put my hand on his arm. "I'm sure things are not as bad as you think. It'll be different when you've been together a little longer."

He started to speak, then stopped as his eyes looked beyond me down the beach. Abruptly he took my hand from his arm and walked away into the woods and I turned and saw his father coming towards me.

"I'd no idea you two were so well acquainted," he said in that sarcastic way of his that I'd come to dislike so much. "In case you're tempted to meddle in what doesn't concern you, perhaps I'd better remind you that you're my secretary and nothing more."

I stared at him coldly and made no answer. He considered me for a while then said, not unkindly, "Peter has a lot of wrong ideas. You mustn't believe them all."

"Do you hate him?"

It was as if I'd hit him in the face. He drew back from me and his eyes opened wide with shock then they blazed with anger.

"How dare you say that?"

"Peter thinks you do."

His face changed again and I saw the hurt look on it that I'd seen in the study when Peter had said he missed his grandfather. "You don't know what you're saying. I told you not to meddle."

"Peter's very unhappy. He needs you. Why do you shut him away?"

I expected an angry rebuff for my persistence but instead I saw the pain deepen in his eyes and for a moment he seemed as hurt and unhappy as Peter himself. Then the old scowling mask came down over his face and his brows drew together.

"Why must you interfere? What do *you* know about anything?"

His scorn filled me with a cold rage so that I no longer cared what I said. "I know what I can see with my own eyes. Your son is lonely and unhappy, and you, his father, turn your back on him. Sometimes I think you must have a devil in you."

I saw his hands clench and his face went white. Without another word he turned and walked swiftly back.

I knew that I'd gone too far, said things that I'd no right to say to him and I was sure that when I returned I should be told to go. I was in no mood to face him yet and I sat down on the beach where I was, going over in my mind what had taken place. I thought of the way he looked when I said that he shut Peter away from him. Yet it must be his fault that the two were at odds. Peter had shown clearly enough that he wanted his father's companionship. Was there some perversity in his nature that made him turn even on those closest to him? I gave it up and after a while returned slowly to the house.

The door was open between our rooms and I saw him standing over by the window.

"You've had a hell of a long lunch hour," he said in a mildly complaining voice as I came in.

"There seemed no point in hurrying. I thought you'd want me to go now."

"On the contrary," he said, turning round. "You're rapidly making yourself indispensable to me."

He stood looking at me with a mildness in his face that matched his voice and, not for the first time, I thought that I would never understand this strange man.

"Well, you've plenty to do, haven't you?" he said brusquely as I stood looking at him.

"There's no reason for hanging around now."

From then on we were back in the friendly atmosphere that we'd worked in before Peter's arrival, although I knew better by now than to take it for granted that we should continue so indefinitely. But in spite of his moodiness, I liked my job and was content to take things as they came.

I didn't see Peter to speak to alone in the next few days but I thought of him a lot and wondered if he were still as unhappy. He seemed cheerful enough when he came down to the boat, but then he always was when in company.

Then one day as I passed the House jetty I saw him examining the sailing dinghy and I went over to speak to him.

"I wish I had someone to sail it with me," he said. "My grandfather often took me out. We'd go for the whole day sometimes and picnic." He gave me a rather embarrassed look. "I'm sorry about the other day. I must have been feeling a bit under the weather."

"Oh, don't worry," I said. "I didn't mind a bit. Sometimes it helps to get things off your chest, anyway. Things never seem so bad when you can talk about them."

"You were right though, about my father

I mean. We're getting on better already."

"Why don't you ask him to go sailing with you?"

"Heavens! What a thought!"

"Why? Can't he swim or something?"

"Oh, he can swim all right. I don't know whether he can handle a boat though. I've never known him to go sailing."

"Well, he can always learn. You must be expert anyway."

He shook his head. "He'd never come."

"Want to bet on it?"

He grinned. "Too unfair. You don't stand a chance."

"All right then. I'll bet you daren't ask him."

He started to laugh. "I can just imagine his face if I did."

"How much then?"

He looked at me for a moment. "You think I won't ask, don't you? Well, I won't fleece you. Make it a shilling."

"All right. A shilling on the asking and two shillings on whether or not he goes."

"That'll be three shillings you'll owe me then."

"Don't count your chickens," I said, but I thought that he was probably right.

A day or so later as we came close to the

island I noticed that the sailing dinghy was missing from the House jetty and when we reached the house Mrs Willis told me that Mr Sutherby would be away all day.

"The two of them have gone sailing," she said. "I was surprised when Peter came and asked if I'd pack them a picnic lunch. He looked so happy too. I'm glad his father's begun to take more notice of him. He was getting almost as moody as his father."

I smiled to myself as I listened to her. So Peter had asked his father and won one bet and I, to my surprise, had won the other, for I hadn't really expected that Mr Sutherby would take him sailing. For Peter's sake I hoped they would have a good day together.

"The boy's doing Mr Sutherby good too," Mrs Willis went on. "I watched them go off. He was almost like a boy himself again. It reminded me of the time he was here as a young man."

I looked at her in surprise. "You knew him as a young man? I didn't even know he'd been to the island before."

She looked a little embarrassed. "I was forgetting myself, though I don't suppose it matters talking about it now. Yes, he came here once to see Fiona. It was a long time ago, before they were married. He was so eager to see her, it seemed such a shame to turn him away."

"Is that what happened?" I asked in astonishment.

"Yes, it was Fiona who'd invited him here, but the master wouldn't agree to it."

"Why didn't he like him?"

"It wasn't that he didn't like him, he didn't know him. But he wanted Fiona to marry someone else and so he had no intention of letting her see him again. There were some rows, I don't mind telling you. Fiona's a lot like her father in some ways. When she's crossed it only makes her more determined to get what she wants. Not that she was any match for her father."

"What happened then, when Mr Sutherby came here, I mean?"

"I'd been told to tell the master if ever he came. They were in the study together for quite a while. I don't know what was said, but the master was in some rage when he rang for me again. I had to fetch Wilson to take Mr Sutherby across in the boat. He looked very angry too and quite white. I felt sorry for him, he'd looked so happy when I'd opened the door to him."

"You mean he didn't see Fiona at all?"

69

Mrs Willis shook her head. "She didn't know he'd been then. After her quarrel with her father she'd written to tell him not to come, so she wasn't expecting him."

I was silent, thinking over what she had told me. I was beginning to see now why Mr Sutherby had so little respect for his father-in-law.

"Good heavens," Mrs Willis said, looking at the clock. "Look how the time's gone on. I mustn't stand chattering any longer. Still, I feel happier today, thinking of the two of them away together."

When I arrived in my room the following day there was a shilling on my desk and I pocketed it with a smile. I heard Mr Sutherby come into the study with a light step and I guessed before I saw him that he was in a good mood. When he called me in for the letters I saw that he was sunburned and his face was more alive than I had yet seen it. I was tempted to ask him if he had enjoyed his sailing, but I had learned that it was better to let him open the conversation, so I kept quiet.

When he had finished dictating he sat looking at me with a look I couldn't fathom. "It was as successful a day as you schemed for," he said at last. Then, as I just sat looking at him, he added, "I asked Peter what gave him the idea of asking me to go sailing with him."

I began to collect up my things, still saying nothing, since I didn't quite know how to reply.

"I seem to remember I asked you once not to meddle in my affairs," he said as I stood up to go. "Perhaps I should remind you again. It doesn't seem to me an unreasonable request."

I had the feeling that in spite of his words he was not displeased and that although he didn't say so he had very much enjoyed his day.

I saw Peter at lunch time and as I walked towards him I took out the shilling and flipped it once or twice into the air.

He grinned. "All right. But it was worth it."

"Did you have a good day?"

"Oh yes. The weather was perfect for sailing. That's what finally pushed me into asking my father before he shut himself up in the study. It was one of the best days I've ever had."

He was silent for a moment, then he said thoughtfully, "I've never been able to get to know my father like that before. I see what

71

you mean about being different underneath. He was great fun. He's almost like two people. I wonder why he's so difficult on the surface?"

I was no more able to answer that question than he was, but I thought that if anyone could mellow Mr Sutherby it would be Peter, for I was convinced that not only did he love his son but he wanted that love returned. Why, in that case, he had kept him at a distance for so long, as Peter said he had, was a mystery to me.

Chapter Five

MR SUTHERBY now spent more and more time with Peter, so that I saw much less of him. He was often away from his room. Sometimes, when they went sailing, as they now frequently did, he was away all day. His writing of the book had slowed almost to a standstill, but there was plenty of back work for me to catch up on when he was missing and the days passed swiftly and peacefully.

When I did see him he was friendly and

good-humoured. His face, without the grim lines or sarcastic look, was quite youthful and attractive and his fine eyes were now alive and warm. His whole manner was more youthful now, for he seemed to have caught some of Peter's zest for life.

I often wondered about his wife, Fiona, especially after what Peter had said about his mother. Sometimes I wondered if she would ever come back to the island. I tried to remember what she had been like when she lived at the House, but I was still a child then and could remember very little. She was only about 19 when she married, immediately after her mother's death. I remembered my father's remark about Peter taking after her and I decided to ask him about her.

"Aye. Young Peter reminds me of her. She was a lively lass."

"Was she very pretty?"

"Aye, that she was. As bonny a lass as you could wish for. Many's the man would have been proud to wed Duncan Reddie's daughter. He had cause enough for anger when she threw herself away like that."

"I think Mr Sutherby must have been very attractive as a young man."

My father was suddenly angry. "Don't

you be getting wrong ideas about that man. You're becoming a deal too friendly. I've seen the two of you walking together. You're a level-headed lass, right enough, but it's my duty to warn you."

"Against what, Father?"

"Now don't you be getting high and mighty with me. People aren't slow to talk. You'll do well to remember your place and keep Mr Sutherby in his."

"Oh let the gossips talk. Mr Sutherby is hardly the type of man to step out of place, as you put it."

"What would you know about him? What kind of principles do you think a man with no religion has? And why do you think his wife's not here with him?"

"Well, it was your idea that I should go to work for him."

"Aye. It was. But I didn't know then that Fiona wasn't to be with him. So you just watch your step."

I had been aware for some time of my father's growing animosity towards Mr Sutherby, or "that man" as he now more often referred to him. When I brought books home from the House he picked them up and looked through them suspiciously. This annoyed me, although I pretended not

74

to notice.

"An interesting book, Father," I said once. "Would you like to read it?"

He looked at me sharply as he put the book down, for although he would often pick up the Bible, he read little else.

"You've always been a sensible lass," he said. "You'll not be changed, I hope, by that man's ideas."

"There can be nothing wrong with liking books and music, surely."

"He'd do better to employ his time more usefully. He wouldn't need to be leaving everything to John Martin then.

"You moon around the house too much," he said presently. "You ought to have some company of your own age. Why don't you go down to the social like Jenny?"

He had never complained of my staying in before. In fact he had been glad of my company and he had told Jenny only recently that she was asking to go out too often.

"You'd not lack for a partner," he went on. "For it's plain to see Rob Davie's set on you. He's a fine enough lad. Why don't you take up with him?" I smiled to myself, thinking that my father must indeed be worried about me to suggest such a thing. He'd never had much praise for Rob before.

I wondered if Jenny was really at the social, although I kept my doubts to myself. She certainly hadn't been to the last one, although she had told my father that was where she was going. Meg had let the cat out of the bag by telling Jenny all about it the next day in front of me.

"Oh well, Ann's not likely to tell on you," she said laughingly when she realised her mistake. Nor did I, but I had spoken to Jenny about it later.

"Oh, you're as bad as Father," she said crossly. "When's he going to realise that I've grown up and don't need watching all the time?"

I was a little uneasy about her, for since my mother's death I felt partly responsible for her. But I didn't want to preach at her for, unlike my father, I now realised that she was rapidly growing up, as she pointed out.

I dismissed my father's opinion of Mr Sutherby as being narrow-minded and unfair. Yet there must be some reason why Fiona didn't come to live with him and I thought about it more and more. I wondered if Mrs Willis knew anything about this and I waited for an opportunity to ask her.

"Peter's holidays will soon be over," she said one day. "His father's going to miss him when he goes back."

"What's he going to do when he leaves school in the summer?" I asked her.

"He'll be going on to University, down in England, I understand."

"Will he come to live here after that, do you think?"

"I've really no idea. When the old master died we were just told that nothing would be changed. Mr Sutherby would be coming to take his place and Peter would be here during his holidays."

"Do you think Mrs Sutherby will be coming to live here soon?"

"That I don't know. Mr Sutherby has never said."

"You knew her well, I suppose, before she was married."

"Aye. I watched her grow up. She was a bonny lass, high spirited too. She was happy enough here till her mother died. That unsettled her. She went away for a while then, down to stay with an old school friend in England. That's when she met Mr Sutherby. When she came back she was full of him but the master was for her marrying a young cousin, or second cousin, of his, Andrew Reddie. He stayed here at the House once or twice. It would have been a good match, I suppose. He was something like the master, only younger, of course. The family name would have been kept here too, which was what the master wanted."

"Well, Fiona got her way, didn't she?"

"Aye. She left the island one day to visit some friends, or so we thought, and she never came back. By the time the master realised what she intended to do it was too late to stop her. He couldn't believe she would do that to him and he never forgave the pair of them. With Peter it was different. He treated him like a son. He'd always wanted a son himself, I suppose that's why he took to the boy."

"It must have all caused quite a stir at the time," I said.

"Aye, there were all sorts of rumours going round, I believe. I knew most of what happened and I was told to keep quiet about it. But it's all over now, with the master being dead too, and I don't suppose it matters any more."

It all sounded very romantic to me and I thought that Fiona must have been very much in love with Mr Sutherby to defy her

78

father as she had. I tried to picture her as she would be now. Around thirty-seven years old with a mature beauty, well-dressed and elegant. How drab she would find everything here. This must be the reason for her not being here now. She knew the life and probably disliked it too much to return to it. I didn't think much of her, all the same, for deserting her husband in this way, for he too had obviously not wanted to come.

For the first time I considered my own appearance. The same jacket and skirt each day with a coat added if the weather was cold. We had always dressed neatly but with economy and until now I had seen nothing wrong with it. Now I thought of Jenny, fussing over her blouses and shoes. She had been ahead of me there too. I wondered if Mr Sutherby thought us all very dreary.

"I suppose we seem terribly old-fashioned and dull here to you," I said to him one day when he'd made some remark about the villagers.

"What is fashion anyway?" he said. "Just a device for making a lot of money out of a lot of silly people, as far as I can see. What's up-to-date today was old-fashioned not so long ago."

He looked at me with a mischievous twinkle. "Perhaps you were looking for an answer in the particular rather than the general. Are you asking me if I think you old-fashioned and dull?"

"Oh no," I said hastily, thinking of all the rude things he'd probably say. "I'm not giving you that chance."

"I'm going to tell you just the same." He paused for a moment, considering me with a little smile.

"Old-fashioned? I suppose you mean in dress. Think what elegant, high-heeled shoes and a close-fitting dress would do to you. You wouldn't roam the island then with the speed and freedom which I've observed. Dull? No, you're not dull, nor ever will be. Don't change for me. I prefer you as you are."

"You're laughing at me, as I knew you would."

"No, I'm not laughing at you. I mean it. Stay as you are."

At times like this when he was friendly or good-humouredly teasing it was difficult to remember the crusty person he had once been. I was very happy there now and I suppose it showed in my face.

"Ann looks so cheerful," Rob said one day

going back in the boat. "I suppose that'll be young Peter taking his father out of her road. The boy's certainly made him a more cheerful character."

"He's a bad influence on the boy," my father said morosely. "They were away up the loch on Sunday with no respect for the Sabbath at all."

I'd seen them too, but it was in the afternoon and Peter had been across to church in the morning, as he still continued to do. Was it really necessary to be as sober and unnatural as my father insisted in order to be religious? I had tried once or twice to talk to him on this question of religion, but he got so angry and upset at my doubts that I now kept such thoughts to myself.

If my father disliked Mr Sutherby already, he was soon to dislike him even more. On a day that was fine and warm I was sitting outside in the sunshine after lunch with Jenny and Meg. Presently Peter came around the side of the house carrying a small radio. He had it tuned low to a programme of records and as he sat on the grass beside us he hummed or whistled snatches of the tunes. Suddenly he leaned over and switched it up louder.

"This is a good one. Listen to the beat."

He started to beat time to the music and Jenny tapped her feet. He looked at her for a moment, then he jumped to his feet.

"Let's dance to it," he said, holding out a hand to pull her up too.

She needed no second invitation and I was surprised to discover how expert she was.

As they were dancing Mr Sutherby came up and Meg immediately got up and disappeared into the house. Jenny stopped dancing when she saw him, but he smiled and told them to carry on. He sat himself down on the low brick wall that edged the grass and I could see that Jenny was embarrassed by his presence. But Peter kept on dancing around her and urging her to join in again and after a moment she overcame her shyness and was soon laughing and dancing with him again.

As I watched them I was filled with envy at their carefree youthfulness and I thought how sober my own life had been since leaving school. Suddenly I felt lonely and apart as if I were already too old to ever feel like them. I looked across at Mr Sutherby, remembering how often I'd thought him lonely. But he didn't look that way now, in fact he seemed to be enjoying himself sitting there watching them. Still, it was different for him, I thought. He hadn't been lonely when he was young. He'd probably laughed and danced with Fiona and been as light-hearted as these two were now.

I was filled with a kind of sadness which I couldn't explain and I felt that I didn't want to sit there watching any longer and thinking such thoughts.

I stood up to go and as I did so he stood up too. "Why should we be left out?" he said, smiling.

Almost before I knew it I was dancing with him and my sadness was forgotten.

"I can't attempt Peter's mad steps," he said, "but we can do something to fit the music."

We'd only been dancing for a minute or so when he suddenly stopped and let me go, looking beyond me with annoyance on his face. I turned round to see what was wrong and saw my father standing watching us, his face dark with anger.

Jenny saw him too and stopped dancing at once, her gaiety all gone. He looked from one to the other of us and for a moment we all stood staring at him. Then Mr Sutherby said curtly, "Well, what is it? What do you want?"

"I'm away to the side garden," my father said slowly, making no attempt to conceal the animosity in his face as he stared at him.

"Well, go on then," Mr Sutherby said sharply, giving him no chance to say more. "Don't stand there looking like God on judgement day."

I saw the colour deepen in my father's face and his knuckles showed white in his clenched fists. I think he was too angry to trust himself to say any more. He glared from one to the other of us again and then turned and walked away.

I was angry myself at his attitude towards us and resentful of his intrusion, for it was impossible now for any of us to recover the happy mood we'd shared. Mr Sutherby was still scowling after his retreating figure and Jenny looked miserable and frightened. Peter bent down and switched off the radio and I went back into the house.

Some time later Mr Sutherby came in. "I'm sorry about what happened just now," he said. "I shouldn't have spoken to your father like that. But by the look on his face he seemed to think we'd all reached the last stages of depravity and it made me very angry."

His face was kind as he looked down at

me and there was a softness in his eyes that suddenly made me feel happy again and I smiled up at him. "It was unfortunate that he came through at that moment."

He gave me a rather rueful little smile. "I hope he will have calmed down before he goes home."

Knowing my father, I thought this was not very likely, yet somehow now I didn't very much care.

Chapter Six

AS my father came down to the boat that evening his face was stern and unsmiling, as I had expected. I arrived only just before him and I had no time to talk to Jenny. I saw her glance swiftly at him as he arrived and then she looked across at me. She looked rather nervous and while he was turned away finding his seat I smiled at her, trying to cheer her up.

I was neither frightened nor repentant. I had done nothing of which I was ashamed and I felt only resentment at his attitude.

I'd given in to him so far without a

struggle and stayed in the village when I wanted to leave. Now I was determined that he was not going to dominate my life in every other respect. I was old enough to think and act for myself and if my ideas didn't always coincide with his he must learn to accept that fact.

Jenny had complained to me more than once of the way he restricted her, thinking that I might stand up for her against him, but until now I'd rather sided with my father, thinking her young enough to need such control. Now I found myself sympathizing with her and I began to understand why she was getting so restive.

My father's silence and sullen face were soon noticed by the others in the boat and they left him alone, not trying to tease him out of it as they might have with someone else, for he was not the easiest of people to get on with at the best of times and they knew better than to provoke him now.

Rob whispered to me, "You'll be having a cheerful evening. Is it your Englishman who's been upsetting him, do you think?" I shrugged as if I didn't know, for I had no intention of discussing the matter with him.

As soon as we landed my father strode off home without waiting for Jenny and me.

"Father's in some mood," Jenny said dejectedly as we followed. "The way he takes on you'd think we were scarlet women."

"Well, we're not. So why worry?" I said cheerfully.

"That's all very well. He'll have plenty to say, just the same, and you know it."

"Well, he won't be the only one. You leave him to me."

She looked at me curiously. "I hope you're as sure of yourself as you look. It's something to have you on my side, at any rate."

When we reached home my father had gone to wash and change from his working clothes as he always did before sitting down to the evening meal. I went into the kitchen to prepare the supper and Jenny followed. My father came back and sat himself down in the living room without a word to either of us and when the supper was ready we took it in and served it out.

It was a miserable meal, for my father sat silent and grim all the way through it. Jenny was nervous and picked at her food and I grew more angry with every uncomfortable minute that passed. There was no point in lingering at such a meal and as soon as we'd finished I stood up to collect the dishes. I intended to clear away the supper things and then have it out with my father. But as Jenny started to help me he stopped us.

"Not so fast. Before you two disappear into the kitchen I want an explanation of that disgraceful behaviour I saw."

I put down the plates I'd picked up and turned to him. "There was nothing disgraceful about it."

For a moment he sat staring at me as if he hadn't heard properly, then he crashed his fist down on the table, making the dishes jump.

"Are you trying to tell me that you see nothing wrong with the way you were all carrying on there?"

"Yes, Father. That's exactly what I am telling you. There was nothing wrong at all with any of our behaviour. It's just what you choose to see in it."

He pushed his chair back violently and got to his feet. I heard Jenny give a little gasp and she moved around the table to my side. I stood my ground, staring defiantly into his angry eyes.

"You clear away the supper things," he said roughly to Jenny. "I'll deal with you later."

Jenny hesitated, but I pushed some dishes into her hands, for this, I knew, was between my father and me.

"What sort of influence do you think you'll be having on that one?" he demanded as she went into the kitchen. "She's a deal too flighty already."

"She's only young," I said, "and that's no crime. Surely there's no harm in wanting a little light-hearted fun?"

"So that's what you call it. Light-hearted fun! Your sister prancing around in front of those two like some hussy and you with a married man's arms around you. A married man who's supposed to be master of the House, and he with his son looking on. What an example to set the boy. Small wonder if he grows up with the wrong ideas in his head. It'll be his father to blame. But I'll not have you two behaving like it."

"Oh, Father, it's your ideas that are wrong. Things have changed since you were young. We were only dancing together and quite openly. It meant nothing to any of us."

"It meant something to me," he said sharply, "and would have done to you before you came under that man's influence. From now on you'll behave as *I* think

89

fitting, make no mistake about that. And that young miss will not be getting so much freedom in the future," he added, jerking his head towards the kitchen.

Then his attack swung back to me. "That man's planted a devil in you. You don't see right from wrong. I've warned you against him before. There's no good in him. I'll not have him corrupt my daughter."

His words ended almost on a shout and his eyes were blazing.

"You're wrong, Father. Your dislike of him makes you see evil in everything he says or does. He's not like you think at all."

"What can a chit of a girl like you know about him? Don't you understand, you little fool, that I'm only trying to protect you?"

"I might understand better if there was something for you to protect me from."

He shook me roughly by the shoulders and then pushed me from him with an exclamation of impatience.

"You wanted to go to work in the town. You'd better look for a job there now."

"I went to work on the island to suit you, but when I leave it will be to suit myself."

He stood over me threateningly. "I'll keep no rebellious daughter under my roof. You'll either respect my wishes or get out."

"I can be independent of you, Father, if you wish it. If I go it will be to live at the House. There's room enough over there for me."

He stood looking at me, breathing heavily. "Aye," he said at last. "I believe you would go there. And that man would be only too ready to take you in."

I don't know what made me think of such a thing and certainly I would not have carried out my threat. It was true that there would be room for me at the House and I would not be the only employee living there, but I would not have wanted to stay there under such circumstances and neither would Mrs Willis be very happy, I knew, to be involved in any way in such a quarrel.

Yet my father obviously thought that I meant what I said and now he was defeated, since the last thing he wanted to do was drive me across to the House.

I think he'd been taken aback by my standing up to him, for such a thing had never happened in our house before. My mother would have cheerfully given in to him rather than spoil the harmony of the home, and Jenny, although she grumbled to me, was too frightened of him still to oppose him. Now he knew that I, at any rate, was

91

not going to be kept under his thumb.

At first he sulked and Jenny was uncomfortable when he was around, but I ignored his mood and behaved as if everything was normal. He couldn't keep it up for ever and even if he did I wasn't going to let it worry me. He gradually came round, but our relationship had changed. There was an uneasy peace between us and both of us were aware that it could easily be broken at any time. All the same, I think he had a new respect for me too.

With Jenny it was a different matter. It seemed that now I had slipped from his control he was making doubly sure that she shouldn't. Under his harshness she grew more and more rebellious although she still dare not show it.

"He makes life a misery," she complained to me. "I'm far happier at work than I am at home."

"And with Tom," I reminded her, trying to cheer her up.

"And precious little time I get with him," she said bitterly. "If he knew about that I suppose he'd want to stop me going out altogether. What does he think life's for?"

"To sew and cook and be seen and not heard, in our case. Most men do, it seems."

"Well Tom's not like that, thank goodness. He's cheerful and good fun. He believes in enjoying life too. He thinks the village is dead and it's people like Father who make it so."

"Why does he stay here if he dislikes it so?"

"You know as well as I do," she said crossly. "He'll be getting his father's business one day. He'll have a say in things then too. Things will be different then, you'll see."

I looked at her with some amusement. "You've certainly been looking ahead, the two of you. And will you be content to stay here too and marry Tom and help to run the village store?"

"Of course I will," she said, her face lighting up at the thought. "There's nothing I want more."

One evening not long after that she was in tears with anger and mortification. She had been a little late in coming home and my father had gone down looking for her.

"If he thinks he'll turn me into a saint by chasing me around he'll soon find out his mistake," she said furiously as we were getting into bed. "If only I could marry Tom and get out."

93

She calmed down after a while and fell asleep and I thought that her mood would have passed by the morning. I felt sorry for her and uneasy, for I knew that my defiance of my father had made things more difficult for her.

He was still apparently unaware of the attachment between her and Tom and I could see that she was now deliberately trying to keep the knowledge from him. Whenever she went out he questioned her closely as to where she was going and what she was going to do, and she never mentioned Tom's name although I guessed that most likely she would be with him. In front of my father in the boat they appeared to be no more than friendly, but before Meg and me they were not worried about keeping their feelings towards each other secret and I saw that Tom was as keen on Jenny as she was on him.

Meg watched the romance grow with great interest and sympathy. "Tom's got eyes for no one else and Jenny never stops talking about him," she said to me one day. "That's what I call love. Jenny'll not be reaching my age before she's married, that's plain to see."

She sounded a little sad and I looked at

her curiously. "Well, I'm older than you and still without a man," I said with a laugh, trying to cheer her up. "You're not on the shelf yet, so don't look so down."

"Ah, but you could have a man for the asking," she said.

I looked at her in surprise, wondering who my secret admirer was. "Who do you mean?"

"Och, away with you, Ann. Are you telling me you haven't noticed Rob's interest in you?"

"Rob!" I said, laughing, then seeing the look on her face I didn't add what I'd been going to say.

"Rob just plays the fool," I said instead. "He'd like us all to think he's the ladies' man. But he's no real interest in me nor I in him."

Suddenly she looked very happy. "You'll be the sly one, I wouldn't wonder," I said. "Getting yourself married off and leaving me on the shelf alone."

She looked at me seriously. "The trouble with you is you're too smart for the village boys. Oh, I didn't mean you look down on them or anything like that," she added hastily. "It's just that somehow you're different, you always have been. You don't seem to really belong in the village, if you see what I mean."

"Well, I'll let you into my little secret," I said, thinking to make it absolutely clear that I would never have any claim on Rob, "I don't intend to stay too much longer. I'd like to get a job in the town."

"Mr Sutherby will miss you if you go," she said. "You get on well with him, don't you? I used to be scared stiff of him, but he's quite a nice man really, isn't he? Of course, he's changed a lot. Must be your influence," she added with a laugh. "Mrs Willis says you act like a charm on him."

"More like Peter who did the charming," I said.

Peter had gone back to school now and I missed him. In fact we all did. His youth and gaiety had brightened up the gloomy old house a lot.

On the day he went back Mr Sutherby moped around for a while, looking very dejected. There was a lingering sadness in his eyes after he'd seen him off that touched me.

"The term will soon go," I said. "Then he'll be here for the summer."

He didn't answer at first. He seemed lost in his thoughts and to have forgotten I was there. Presently he said quietly, almost as if speaking to himself:

"He was always a high-spirited child. I used to watch him at play with his friends. If he knew I was there he'd become nervous and embarrassed. He's quite natural with me now. At last he's discovered I'm human."

Then he looked directly at me. "You know, it's you I have to thank for that too. You've been softening me up ever since you came here, haven't you?"

He was half-teasing, half-serious as he looked at me. "Don't you realise, my little meddler, that I'm actually trying to thank you for it now?"

I felt a sudden deep warmth for him and I smiled at him. "I'm glad," I said.

"You know, I actually dreaded Peter coming here," he said. "You wouldn't understand that, but it's true. But never again. No, never again."

He looked happy again and presently he said briskly, "Well, let's get back to work. I've been rather neglecting it lately."

Chapter Seven

MR SUTHERBY now went back to his writing of the book and he was in his study for most of each day. Our days began to take on a regular pattern. He would deal with the business of the estate first, as quickly as possible, and then turn to his real interest, the manuscript.

His desk was strewn with books of reference and piles of scribbled notes, for he had had access to many letters and papers relating to his subject. Apart from the typing, I was able to help him quite a bit in getting his material sorted out and arranged and I became almost as absorbed in it as he was. We worked long hours side by side, often to a background of music.

He told me about the places he'd visited and people he'd met while carrying out his research and I never tired of listening to him. I envied Fiona sharing such a life with him.

"What an interesting life you have," I said to him once. "That's how I'd like to live."

He gave me a strange look and for a while he didn't answer.

"Well at least I can take my writing with

me wherever I go," he said at last. "How else could I have faced my imprisonment here?"

"I'm sorry you look on the island like that," I said.

He gave me a teasing smile. "Oh, it's improved so much since I first came here. Far more than I could ever have imagined. I'm almost beginning to be happy here. But then, you see, I have a most charming fellow prisoner, and I'm relieved to see she's not in quite such a hurry to escape as I was at first led to believe."

I smiled too as I thought of our first meeting. It was difficult now to believe he was the same person.

"If I'd known I should find *you* here I would not have been so reluctant to come back to the island."

He still had the teasing smile on his lips, yet there was a softness in his face and eyes that made me feel he more than half meant what he said. I was aware of a warm feeling between us, a deeper friendliness.

"I hadn't realised you had been to the island before," I began and then stopped short, remembering what delicate ground I was on. I expected that he would change the subject or perhaps fall into one of his silent moods, but although his face changed, losing its softness, he answered me.

"Yes, I've been here before. For a brief visit."

He gave a little harsh laugh. "Very brief in fact. Even so, I doubt if it went unnoticed in that village of yours. But you would have been just a child."

With a sudden movement he pushed his chair back and stood up and walked over to the fireplace. When he turned to face me he was a different person from the teasing, gentle one of a few minutes before. His face was hard and his eyes full of a dark anger.

"Yes, I came to the island," he said. "And I met my future father-in-law. He allowed me to stay long enough to tell me that he considered me an adventurer, hoping to raise myself up the social scale by marriage with his daughter, and looking for a life of ease at his expense."

I gave a little gasp and, crossing the floor, he rested his hands on the desk and leaned towards me.

"You accused me of having no respect for the dead. I had no respect or liking for him when he was alive. Why should I pretend now? Does death turn him into a saint or wipe out the memory of him as he lived?"

Looking into his face I saw how deeply he had been hurt; how the scar had never healed.

"I'm beginning to understand," I said.

"Beginning, yes, only beginning," he said. "For that day was only the beginning. You haven't heard the half of it."

He turned away from me and began restlessly to move about the room. I could sense the passion that was bottled up inside him and I wondered what that other half, that I didn't know about, could be. I sat in silence, watching him. I felt that he had already confided in me more perhaps than he had intended and I had no wish to intrude further.

Presently he came back and perched himself on the desk. With an attempt at a smile he nodded towards the picture over the fireplace.

"I found little pleasure in seeing *him* up there on the wall."

"You were right to change the room round," I said, with a smile to answer his own. "Even I will admit that now."

I looked around at all the things that belonged to him, his gramophone, records, books and pictures.

"The room belongs to you now. I like it

much better the way it is."

He had recovered himself completely again and was looking at me with his teasing smile.

"That's quite a victory for me," he said. "At last I have won your approval and you have no idea what that means to me."

Again I had the feeling that although he was teasing, he half meant what he said. I felt a blush coming to my face and to hide it I stood up and went across to the fireplace.

"I like this painting," I said, looking up at it. "It's such a pretty little village. Is it a real place?"

He came over and stood beside me. "Yes, it is. It was painted by a friend of mine. I was born in that village. My father was vicar of that church."

"Vicar!"

He shrugged, half impatiently. "Vicar, minister, priest. Does it matter what you call them?"

"It wasn't the name that surprised me," I said.

"What then?" he demanded with some of his old aggressiveness.

"Well, you never go to church . . . ."

"No, I never go to church," he took me up as I hesitated. "Not since I quarrelled with my father, over religion, or rather his idea of religion. He couldn't bear to listen to what he considered blasphemy from his own flesh and blood. And I couldn't keep my ideas to myself however much I hurt him."

"I'm sorry," I said, for his voice sounded full of regret. "I'm glad you told me, though. In a way it's a comfort for me to know because I can't really believe a lot of the things I've been brought up to believe in. But it's impossible to talk to my father about it."

He gave me a little smile of amusement. "I suppose your father believes in hell-fire, eternal damnation and the lot."

"Do you believe in God?"

"I don't believe in the God I suspect your father believes in. A Being conceived in man's own image. A kind of all-powerful manipulator sitting somewhere outside the world controlling all his puppets."

"But there must be something beyond this life, some reason for us being here."

"The answer to that can only be speculated upon. For my part it's as much as I can manage to cope with this life, without worrying about the hereafter."

It was a relief to be able to say to him what I couldn't say to my father and now I found that, apart from his private affairs, he would discuss any subject quite freely with me. We resumed our lunch time walks which we had dropped while Peter was on the island and on these walks we had many discussions, when I forgot the difference in years between us and the fact that he was master of the House, for he talked as if we were equals.

Inevitably we returned to the subject of religion, for I had worried about it for some time. When we went into it more deeply I discovered that the opinions he held were very sincere, if unorthodox, and that he had not arrived at his conclusions lightly. I admired him for not accepting any ready-made formulae where he found he could not agree with them.

"Every thinking person searches for the truth at some time or other," he said, "and everyone has the right to his own beliefs. So don't let your father, or anybody else for that matter, impose his will on you against your better judgment."

He was silent for a while and as I walked beside him I saw his face darken. "No. Don't let anybody else lead your life for you. For then you become what you shouldn't be. You are nobody. You are a misfit."

I knew as I looked at him that he was no longer thinking about me or my problems. His face had set into a mask of bitterness and his eyes stared glassily ahead. Abruptly he turned and walked towards the house and I followed in silence, wondering what memories plagued him, shut away there in his own secret world.

These moods would come upon him from time to time, brought on by some chance remark that pushed him back into the past. There was still a lot about him that I didn't understand, things that had affected him very deeply that I couldn't even guess at.

But these moods made no difference to the friendship that was now firm between us and I began to think that at last he was content to be living on the island. Then one day as we were walking in the woods I stopped beside a hawthorn tree to sniff the sweet scent of the may blossom.

"I can never make up my mind which time of the year I like best," I said rather dreamily as we walked on again. "I love the early spring when everything's coming to life again and I love days like this when the trees are full out and the loch seems asleep under the sun. But the autumn's beautiful too, when the trees are changing and the hills are coloured with the heather and bracken. And so is the winter when the hills are snow-capped and everything's sparkling with ice and frost. The soft days are lovely and the wild ones are too, when the wind goes mad in the trees and whips a fury into the water."

He had been walking in front, parting the branches for me to pass through and I wondered if he was even listening to me, for I was talking to myself. But now he stopped and turned round to look at me.

"If anyone could make me find this place attractive it would be you. You're so much a part of it, part of its unspoiled beauty."

He looked at me for a moment with that half-teasing, half-tender look that I had begun to find so disturbing, then his face changed and he said, "No. Not even you could make me do that."

I watched the shadows gather in his face and he turned back and walked on. But when we came out of the woods to the beach he appeared to have forgotten his dark thoughts, whatever they were. I noticed that, as time went by, he seemed able to shake himself out of his moods more quickly.

If there was a serenity now about my days on the island, it was not so at home. My quarrel with my father had built a barrier between us and however much I tried to ignore it we were no longer entirely comfortable in each other's presence. And I was by no means happy about Jenny.

At first I thought that her angry rebelliousness would have to explode and I was afraid of the outcome. Then she quietened down, but I knew this wasn't because she had decided to resign herself to her lot. There was something about her quietness that worried me. I noticed the strained atmosphere between herself and Tom and she no longer laughed and fooled with Meg.

Meg was worried too. "What's the matter with Jenny?" she asked me. "Has she quarrelled with Tom? I know there's something wrong, but she won't tell me. She told me to mind my own business when I asked her. It's not like her to be so sharp."

I watched her with Tom in the boat going home. She sat silent and listless, all her old animation gone. Tom was obviously unhappy and from the way he kept looking at her I could see that his feelings towards her hadn't changed. If they had quarrelled, I thought, it was not his fault that they hadn't made it up. She would tell me nothing, saying only that I was imagining things.

Then one evening at the supper table she pushed her plate away untouched, saying that she wasn't hungry. Her face was full of strain and her fingers drummed nervously on the table.

"Why don't you go to bed?" I suggested. "You're not looking well."

She glanced at my father, but he went on eating his supper and said nothing, and after a moment she left the table and went upstairs.

"You shouldn't give in to her moods," he said after she'd gone.

"Moods!" I answered sharply. "Can't you see that she's not well?"

"She'll have forgotten all about it by the morning," he said calmly.

When I went up to see her she was huddled down in bed with the sheet pulled up around her face. I stood beside the bed looking at her and as she didn't speak to me I turned the sheet gently back to see if she was sleeping. I saw that she'd been crying and I knelt down beside the bed.

"Jenny, what's the matter? Can't you tell me?"

She shook her head miserably.

"I only want to help you."

"Nobody can help me," she said and she began to cry again, burying her head in the pillow.

I smoothed the hair back from her forehead and took one of her hands in mine, trying to comfort her.

"Father will be shouting up if you don't go down," she said after a while.

"Let him shout," I said. "I can't go and leave you like this. I wish there was something I could do."

"You'd better go," she said, after another pause. "I don't want him coming up here."

"All right," I said, seeing her uneasiness. "But I'll be back soon. I'll come up to bed early."

When I went upstairs again she'd fallen into a restless doze and I got quietly into bed trying not to disturb her. I lay there for a long time before I got to sleep myself, worrying about her and wondering what was wrong.

In the morning she was already out of bed when I woke up, but she looked very pale and there were great shadows under her eyes. She said she felt a little sick and wouldn't want any breakfast. I told her to get back into bed, but she wouldn't listen to me.

"Father will pester me with questions if I stay home. I'll be all right," she said.

I left her sitting on the edge of the bed while I went down to get the breakfast. She was still upstairs when it was time for us to leave. I heard my father call up to her as he waited impatiently at the door and I came through from the kitchen to insist that she stay home and go back to bed. She was at the head of the stairs when I reached the bottom and I saw her suddenly double up as if in pain. I rushed up the stairs, afraid that she was going to fall down them.

My father came up behind me. "What ails the lass?" he asked in an anxious voice as we helped her back into the bedroom. Even in my anxiety for Jenny I was struck by the worry in his face and the gentleness now in his voice. He stood uncertainly by the bed as she lay on it.

"She'll be all right, Father. I'll stay and take care of her. You'd best be going if you're to catch the boat. They'll not hold it much longer. Can you get a message in to the doctor for me, then I'll not need to leave her. And will you ask Meg to tell Mrs Willis. She'll tell Mr Sutherby."

"Aye, lass. If there's nothing I can do, I'd best be off. I'll get word to the doctor for you."

Our shared anxiety had brought us together again and I rested my hand on his arm as he went to the door.

"Don't worry, Father. She'll be all right."

"Aye, lass. She's in good hands. I know that well enough."

I turned back to the bed. Jenny was lying with her eyes closed and every now and again her face twisted with pain and she gave a little gasp. She had been dressed ready to go to work and now I helped her out of her clothes and tucked her back into bed. There was little else I could do until the doctor came, and I sat beside the bed watching her, nagged now by a suspicion that I hardly dared acknowledge.

I was relieved to hear the doctor's knock on the door and I hurried down to let him in.

Dr Steven was a cheerful and kindly man whom we knew very well as he'd attended my mother all through the long years of her illness, and Jenny and me for our childish complaints. I also happened to be the first baby he delivered as a young doctor new to the village, a fact which he said gave him a fatherly interest in me.

"What's young Jenny been up to?" he said. "Your father thinks it's appendicitis, but I'd be as well maybe to make my own diagnosis."

I took him up to the bedroom and watched him while he bent over Jenny for a minute or two. He gave me a curious look.

"Will you be heating some water. I'll come down when I'm ready for it."

I went downstairs to wait for him in the kitchen, still with that foreboding at the back of my mind. I guessed that he had sent me from the bedroom in order to talk to Jenny alone and now I could hear the murmur of his deep voice.

"What is it?" I said when he came down. "What is the matter with her?"

Again he gave me that curiously searching look.

"Don't you know, Ann?"

I shook my head.

"She was going to have a baby."

I felt the colour go from my face, for this is what I'd begun to suspect and dread.

"I can see you didn't know," he said as he watched me, "and neither, of course, does your father."

He started to collect up the things he needed.

"Will she be all right?" I asked.

"Yes. She'll be all right. She'll lose the baby, which is probably a good thing under the circumstances. I'm afraid she'll have to go into the hospital for a day or two."

He turned to go back upstairs and I started to follow him.

"There's nothing you can do at the moment," he said, stopping me. "I'll call you if I need anything. Why don't you make yourself some tea. I can see this has been a bit of a shock to you."

I turned back into the kitchen, remembering my father's anxious face that morning. His concern for Jenny would soon turn to something very different when he found out the truth.

Chapter Eight

I SAT in the kitchen waiting for Dr Steven to call me, my mind going round and round in the same unhappy circle. Always it came back to my father. He had been right about

Jenny and I had been wrong. Added to my dread of his reaction to the news was a feeling of guilt at the part I had played. I had deliberately withheld from him the knowledge of Jenny's meetings with Tom, which I had long guessed at; the knowledge that might well have prevented this happening. This thought and the thought of facing him, together with my worry over Jenny, were as crushing as some physical force so that I couldn't bring myself to move.

I heard Dr Steven moving about overhead and his deep voice talking to Jenny, and at last he came down.

"She'll be all right," he said, answering my look as I roused myself to meet him. "But you must understand this whole business has been a great strain on her, mentally and emotionally. I want her kept quiet and not excited in any way. She's in a highly nervous state. I've given her a sedative and she'll probably sleep for a while. Later on, if she wants to talk to you, let her, it'll do her no harm to get a few things off her chest, but don't press her. I'll arrange with the hospital to send out an ambulance, she'll need to go in for a day or two, as I said. I'll call in on my afternoon round to let you know if they can take her today."

After he'd gone I went upstairs to look at Jenny to assure myself that she was asleep and needed nothing. Her long lashes lay darkly on her pale face and her hair spread over the pillow. I was filled with pity as I bent over her, she looked so young. I wondered if she would ever again be the light-hearted girl she'd been such a short time back.

She slept for quite a while and when she woke I took her in something to eat and sat beside her. She seemed quite drowsy still, then suddenly she sat right up in the bed with a look of panic on her face.

"What am I going to do?" she asked me in a voice full of desperation.

"It's all right," I said. "You've nothing to worry about now except getting better."

"But how can I face anyone again after this?" Her eyes were enormous as she stared at me.

"Don't be a goose," I said. "Nobody knows, unless you've told anyone."

She shook her head. "What about Father, does he know?"

"Not yet," I said.

She began to sob wildly and I put my arm round her shoulders and tried to soothe her.

"You're not to worry about Father. I'll speak to him. In any case, you may not even be here when he comes home. You know you have to go into hospital for a day or so?"

She nodded. "Everyone will know then," she sobbed.

"Of course they won't. There's no reason why anyone should know why you've gone. I'll think of something to tell them. You just go away quietly and get yourself well. You'll be able to face things much better then. And father will have had time to cool off too."

"He'll never forgive me for this. Though it was all his fault. He drove me to it. I just wanted to show him that his bullying didn't get him anywhere. I didn't care if I did have a baby. I thought I'd have to get married then. But when I knew it had happened I was frightened. I didn't want to go through with it."

She choked on her tears and I made another attempt to calm her. "Well you're not going to have the baby and now you've got to put the whole thing behind you. You're not to upset yourself any more."

She was quiet for a while, then she said, "Tom will be wondering what's the matter

116

with me. I wouldn't tell him about the baby," she added, seeing my look of surprise. "I didn't want him to go to Father."

"Well, he must have known something was wrong. He couldn't fail to see it if he thinks anything of you."

"He just thinks I've turned against him . . . after what happened. I wish I could see him again.

"I know what you're thinking," she said when I didn't answer. "But you're wrong. Tom's not to blame. It was all my fault."

Remembering Dr Steven's advice not to excite her, I let that go. "Try to rest again now," I said, attempting to settle her back in the bed.

She seized hold of my hand and looked at me with a wildness in her eyes that frightened me. "Father mustn't know it was Tom. I'll not tell him that. You'll not tell him either? Promise me you won't ever tell him. If he tries to stop me seeing Tom I'll . . . I'll kill myself."

"Oh, Jenny, such wild talk! It's bad for you to excite yourself like this . . ."

"Promise then. Promise you won't tell," she said, still clutching my hand and resisting my efforts to settle her down again.

"All right. I promise. And now lie down

and rest. The sooner you get yourself better the sooner you'll see Tom again."

I promised what she asked in order to calm her down and there seemed no reason not to. I thought my father would guess soon enough who it was without any help from me, for once he started to think about the matter his suspicions were bound to rest on Tom.

She let me lay her back on the pillow and I tucked the bedclothes around her. "All you must think about now is getting better," I told her again. "If you and Tom really love each other, you'll be getting married one of these days and neither father nor anyone else will be able to stop you. So just think about that."

I sat by the bedside with her, but she showed no more inclination to talk. After a while she closed her eyes and soon I knew that she'd fallen asleep again. My thoughts were bitter as I watched her, for I felt that this would never have happened if my mother had been alive. She blamed my father's harshness for her recklessness. I'd increased that harshness by setting myself against him, and by my tacit acceptance of her behaviour I'd encouraged her recklessness. She had been foolish, no doubt, but we were not blameless either.

Now it seemed to me that the only sensible thing to do was to bury the past between us, each taking our lesson from it. But the more I thought about my father, the more certain I was that he would never see things as I saw them. As Jenny had said, he would never forgive her nor would he believe that his own behaviour had anything to do with it. She had sinned against him, against all decent society, against God even. He would not be willing to forgive or forget this. His harshness would increase if anything, nor would he be much different towards me if he saw I had any sympathy for her. No matter how repentant Jenny might be now, how could she face such a future without being driven to desperation again. The thought nagged me all the time until I was near to desperation myself.

I was still worrying about it when Dr Steven came back.

"The ambulance will be out this evening," he said. "If you like to go in with Jenny, I'll bring you back home. I'll be in there later. How's she been?"

"She's slept most of the time, but she woke up once and we had quite a long talk."

119

He nodded with satisfaction. "I'm glad that she feels she can talk to you. It's not good for her to keep it all to herself. You know, Ann, no matter what you think about this business, it's sympathy and understanding she needs now. Somebody to help her get back her composure."

"Yes, I understand," I said. "But I'm not sure that my father will."

He looked at me thoughtfully. "I've been thinking the same. Your father's going to take this very hard. He has very strict ideas of right and wrong. I'm afraid Jenny's behaviour in his eyes will be inexcusable."

"My father needn't know about the baby. Nobody else does. I'll think of some other explanation for Jenny's illness. I think it will be better if he doesn't know the truth."

"What are you thinking of telling him?" he asked sharply. "You must know that I'll not back you up in a lie."

"There'll be no need." My father's voice spoke from the doorway, sending a shock through me. I'd lost all sense of time and I had not heard his key in the lock.

He started to move into the room. "No need for any more lies. For now I see the truth only too plainly. One of my daughters no better than a whore. The other a liar and

120

cheat who is well on the way to becoming the same."

I shrank away from him as he spat the last words into my face.

Dr Steven moved swiftly to the door and closed it.

"Control yourself, man," he said sharply. "I can well understand your anger and upset, but you'll do no good by behaving like this. Jenny is in a state of emotional shock. Any harshness or violence on your part could have a very bad effect on her."

My father turned on him with blazing eyes. "You seem to have forgotten she's my daughter."

"I'm aware of that. Even so, until your anger has cooled down you'd better stay away from her. Remember, Mr Carroll, however wrongly and foolishly Jenny has behaved, she has not gone through this without suffering. It was through compassion for her that Ann felt driven to lie to you. Can you not also find a little compassion?"

My father stared at him in silence for a minute or two, then he said slowly, "Aye. She may have suffered, which is no more than she deserves. But does he suffer?"

He turned on me and repeated his

question violently. "Does he suffer?"

The look in his eyes made me despair for Tom's chances with Jenny, for it seemed he'd already guessed who was concerned.

Dr Steven went up to take a look at Jenny, but came down immediately to say that she was still sleeping. When I'd shown him out, I went into the living room where my father was standing and closed the door behind me.

"You've known about this all along." His hard eyes glowered at me.

"No, Father. I didn't know until Dr Steven told me this morning."

"You're lying still," he said harshly. "Just as you've lied about him all along. You lie to your own father to cover up for *him*."

"No matter what you think, Father, I am not in the habit of lying. Nor is there any need for me to cover up for anybody. I was prepared to lie to you this once, it's true, but only to save Jenny from any more upset."

"Your concern for your sister does you little credit. It's a pity you didn't think of it before and discourage her from such association instead of encouraging her. I know well enough why you didn't want me

122

to know. So that's your virtuous, respectable man."

"That's unfair, Father. You don't even try to understand."

"Understand," he shouted. "I understand only too well. You're already so corrupted you don't even care what he is. One thing's certain. Jenny'll not set foot on the island again. You'll not either, unless you want to end up as she has. Or is my warning already too late?"

I stared back at him appalled. I had thought all along he was talking about Tom. Now at last I realised what he was thinking.

"Oh no, Father. How can you think such things?"

"Don't put on a show of virtue for me. Isn't there proof enough upstairs?"

"You can't believe Mr Sutherby is responsible. Oh no, Father, much as you dislike him, even you can't believe that."

"Him, or his son. What's the difference? For it's plain to see that young Peter's come under his evil influence just as you seem to be. Do you think this would have happened if his grandfather had still been master of the House? You know very well it wouldn't. The boy would have been kept in his rightful place and you and Jenny in yours."

"How can you be so blind, so unfair, Father? Peter's certainly not the kind of person you seem to think he is. How little you know either him or his father."

"I know his father only too well. I've watched the way you've changed since you've been in his company. And the boy's changed too. It was a sad day for him when his grandfather died. He was like a father to him. His own father wasn't fit to bring him up. See what happens to him now, after a few short weeks of *his* influence."

"You're wrong, Father. So wrong. Neither Peter nor his father had anything to do with this affair."

"Then since you know so much about it, perhaps you'll tell me who *is* responsible. Well, come on. Who is it?"

He laughed scornfully when I didn't answer.

"Your silence speaks for itself. I was beginning to think there was no end to the lies you'd tell for him. At least you'll not stoop to blame an innocent person."

"It's you who are blaming an innocent person, but you won't face up to the truth."

He grabbed my arm and pulled me towards the door. "We'll see who's to blame. We'll hear the truth from her own lips. Perhaps then you'll not deny it."

I pulled away from him in alarm. "No, Father. Remember what Dr Steven said. Jenny's not to be upset."

He stood looking at me with a scornful smile, his hand resting on the door knob.

"One excuse is as good as another. Now who won't face the truth?"

I turned hopelessly away. No matter what he believed, I wouldn't drag Jenny into the quarrel.

He came back into the room and stood behind me. "You know as well as I do that it was young Peter. And don't you think his father doesn't know. No doubt he's laughing at the foolish girl . . . my daughter . . . who was a good enough lass until he came here. Laughing at me, her father, who's striven to bring you both up as God-fearing young women. Laughing to think I've failed. It's like the Devil himself sitting over there in the House."

His voice was shaking with passion. I turned to face him and the look in his eyes terrified me. I shrank before such hatred; hatred which I knew was undeserved.

"May God forgive you," I whispered.

"God," he thundered. "What right have you to ask God's forgiveness for me? You with your doubts and blasphemies . . . your deceits and your lies. You should be on your knees asking forgiveness for yourself. But I suppose you're already beyond that. Soon you'll not be setting foot inside the church. Soon you'll be as black a heretic as he is himself, that man you so righteously defend."

"If I turn away from the church, Father, it will be through you and not Mr Sutherby. He may not believe as you do, yet he is a kind and honourable man. Your religious beliefs seem to allow no understanding nor compassion. Your mind is twisted and filled with hatred. How can I follow such an example?"

He caught hold of me, and the grip of his hands bruised my arms.

"That man has hypnotized you. He could twist you round his finger. If he called you now, you'd go running to him, wouldn't you?" He shook me furiously. "Wouldn't you?"

Suddenly my control broke. "Yes, I would," I shouted at him. "Yes, I would." Then I added, almost in tears and scarcely aware of what I was saying. "If only I could."

My father let go of me and raising his

hand gave me a stinging slap across the face. I swayed under the blow and fell back into a nearby chair. I sat there, staring in front of me, clutching the arms of the chair, frozen with shock. Not the shock of the blow, although my face was smarting, but the shock of the realization that the words I'd spoken in desperation were true. If Mr Sutherby called me to him, I would go running, with a wild happiness. If I could feel his arms around me nothing else would ever matter again.

My father was right. He *could* twist me round his finger if he wanted to. For now I knew that I loved him.

Chapter Nine

I DON'T know how long I sat there in the living room, for there was a timelessness about my thoughts that seemed to lift me out of this world. I did not notice my father leave the room, although I was aware of him coming once to stand and look at me. He was washed and changed from his working clothes then, so time must have passed. Still

I sat on as if in a dream.

A knock at the front door roused me and brought me back to the reality of the present. I knew it would be the ambulance arriving to take Jenny to the hospital, and I went to open the door.

When I took the attendant into the bedroom Jenny was awake and she eyed him rather nervously. I guessed that now the time had come to go she was a little frightened, for she hadn't been into hospital before.

"I'm coming with you to see you settled in," I said, trying to reassure her. "There'll be nothing to worry about and you'll be home again in no time at all."

"I'm glad you're coming with me," she said. "Everything seems so unreal. I keep wondering if it's really happening."

My father didn't come to see us off or give any word of comfort to Jenny and as I climbed into the ambulance beside her I found it a great effort to appear cheerful.

The hospital was some distance away in the small town of Tollie, where I had gone to school. It was a small cottage hospital with a friendly, informal atmosphere.

As soon as Jenny had been put to bed I was allowed to go in and sit with her until

Dr Steven was ready to take me home. There were four other patients in the same room, two of whom were walking around. One of these was a young girl of around Jenny's age who was obviously pleased to have her in the same room. They were all chattering away and it wasn't long before they drew Jenny into their conversation too, although she was still very quiet.

Presently a young nurse came in to take temperatures and there was a lot of teasing and leg-pull. I watched a slow smile come to Jenny's face. She was going to be all right here; better off for a few days in this cheerful company than she would be in the present atmosphere at home.

Going back in the car Dr Steven said something to the same effect. "She'll be a lot better by the time she returns home. If your father can bring himself to accept the situation there'll be no harm done."

I thought about Jenny's problems as we drove along, wondering what the immediate future would be like for her once she was home. Even if she's unhappy for a while, I thought, she'll be better off than me in the end. At least she's in love with somebody who loves her and some day she'll be able to marry him. For me there was no such happiness. The man I loved was already married and certainly he had shown no sign of love for me. Gentleness, kindness, friendly companionship too, but never anything more. No matter what my father chose to imagine, he had never been other than Mr Sutherby, my employer.

I was in no mood for conversation, and Dr Steven, probably sensing my mood, gave his attention to steering the car along the winding, narrow roads.

It was a fine evening and the countryside looked beautiful, all the colours heightened in the late sun. As we neared the village the loch showed calm and silvery beneath the sky that held varying shades of pink and yellow and blue. The island lay like a green oasis on its desert of water, the chimneys of the House distinct in the clear light. How near it looked. How near I was to the strange man I had come to love and yet how far away he really was, how inaccessible to me.

Dr Steven helped me from the car and held my hand for a moment as I thanked him for bringing me home. His face was full of kind concern.

"Try not to worry. Jenny's young. She'll soon put all this behind her. Today has been a great strain for you. Now go and get some rest yourself."

I let myself into the house, remembering only now that I had done nothing about the supper, but when I went into the kitchen I saw that my father had helped himself. I cleared away the things he'd left and went to find him. He was sitting in the living room with a book on his lap and I guessed it was the Bible.

"I see you've had some supper," I said. "I'm very tired. I'm going to bed."

He made no answer to this, nor did he ask me about Jenny. He gave me a strange look as I said goodnight and something in his look hurt me. I think he was as shaken by the day's events as I was myself. We'll never be close again, I thought, as I slowly climbed the stairs. This time we've gone too far apart.

The bedroom seemed strangely empty without Jenny, yet I was glad to be alone. I sat on her bed for a moment or two, thinking about her, and then inevitably my thoughts came back to my own situation.

I went over to the window and, pushing it wide, I sat down beside it and looked across to the island, remembering the happy days I had spent there.

My mind went back over the past months since I had first gone to work for Mr Sutherby. How had I come to love him, for our first meetings had held neither warmth nor friendliness? I remembered him as he was in those early days, prickly, brusque, rude even. Somehow, somewhere, I had come to know the warm, attractive person beneath the frowning exterior.

At first I had thought of him as much older than myself, but lately there had seemed little difference between us. I suppose I was old for my years, for I seemed to have skipped my teens. My mother's illness, the knowledge that she would never recover and the shifting of the household responsibilities to my shoulders had changed me from a schoolgirl to a young woman in outlook if not in years, so that with people of my own age I felt old and staid. With Mr Sutherby now I felt young and lighthearted and yet at the same time closer in years and more in sympathy with him than someone of my own age, like Rob.

The thought of Rob kissing me, holding me in his arms, filled me with revulsion. Yet the thought of Mark Sutherby taking me in his arms filled me with such a longing that I could no longer hold back the tears. Resting my arms on the window ledge, I buried my head in them and sobbed until my head throbbed and no more tears would come.

When at last I raised my head the light had gone from the sky and the island was now only distinguishable as a dark smudge on the light surface of the water. I remembered how I'd looked across to it on the evening before I first went to work there. How I'd wondered if it would trap me, keeping me back from the life I wanted to lead. Now I knew that it held everything I wanted from life. Now I would have to leave it, but part of myself would be left behind. The island and the House, because they held Mark Sutherby, had trapped my heart and would keep it, wherever I went, whatever I did.

Mark. I said his name over and over, wanting to call him by it. For now he was no distant employer to me, no master of the island. Here in the loneliness of my room it didn't matter how much I gave way to my feelings. But before I faced him again I must be in control of myself, for he must never know what I felt for him.

I turned from the window, almost too exhausted to undress. I was too tired to think any more and almost as soon as I was in bed I fell into a heavy sleep.

The alarm clock woke me, ringing loudly in my ears. Usually I had no difficulty in waking up, and set the alarm only as a precaution. My eyes felt stiff and puffy as I struggled to open them and my head was heavy and my throat dry. I was thankful that I was not going to work, for I had arranged to go and see Jenny later in the day. I would have to go into Tollie on the bus that brought the schoolchildren home, and if I crossed to the island I would not be home in time to catch it.

"I'll not be coming with you today," I told my father as I put his breakfast on the table. "I'm going to see Jenny later on. I'll be gone before you get home, but I'll leave your supper ready for you in the oven."

He had not spoken to me yet, although I had caught him looking closely at me once or twice. Now he just grunted and gave me no message for Jenny.

Later in the morning I went into the village to do some shopping and everybody I met asked me how Jenny was and what was wrong with her, for by now the whole village knew that she had gone into hospital. I told them enough to satisfy their curiosity without admitting to the whole truth. By the time she came home she would not have to face any awkward questions.

I had thought to straighten out my tangled thoughts as I sat in the bus on my way to the hospital, for I had not been able to do so while working about the house. One thing was clear. I must leave the island as soon as possible and leave the village too. Only in a completely new life could I hope to put the past behind me. But I couldn't go until Jenny had settled down again and was able to carry on without me. How long would this take?

She was lying back on the pillows with her eyes closed when I went into the room and she still looked very pale. But she opened her eyes as I bent over her, and smiled at me.

She said she was doing fine. "Everybody's so kind and friendly," she added. "In fact I'm dreading coming home now."

"Everybody in the village knows you're in here, of course, and they all wish you well. They won't bother you with questions though, so don't be afraid of that." I told her what I had told the people I met while I was shopping that morning.

"It's Father I'm frightened of. I keep thinking what it's going to be like when I

135

get home. What did he say when he found out?"

"Well, he had plenty to say, of course. And naturally it was a great shock to him. But he'll be over the worst of it by the time you get home."

She shook her head. "Thanks for trying to cheer me up. But I know Father. Has he said anything about Tom?"

"No. He hasn't mentioned Tom."

She looked at me quickly. "But he asked who it was. That'd be one of the first things he would ask. You didn't tell him?"

"No," I said slowly. "I didn't tell him."

She took my hand and squeezed it. "I don't know what I would have done if it hadn't been for you.

"It isn't any use though," she said after a while. "He's bound to guess." She turned her head away from me and closed her eyes and I watched the tears trickle from under her eyelids.

"I don't think he will guess. I don't think he'll ever know unless you tell him. He thinks it happened on the island."

Her eyes opened wide in disbelief. "Who could he possibly suspect?"

I couldn't bring myself to tell her. I didn't want to talk about either Peter or his father just then.

"Does it matter? I didn't say anything because I'd promised you I wouldn't. He says you're not to go back to work at the House again. If you can find yourself a job in the village and do as he wants, I don't suppose he'll even ask you. But I think when you've got over all this, when you feel more sure of yourself, you ought to tell him the truth."

The knowledge that Tom was under no suspicion from my father cheered her up and I stayed talking to her for quite a while.

"I'm sorry about all this," she said as I said goodbye. "Leaving you to face Father and everything. I'll never forget the way you've stood by me."

I bent down to kiss her and she held me close for a moment, looking intently into my face.

"You look worn out and you've great dark circles under your eyes. Was it very awful?"

"I'm just tired, that's all," I said quickly. "I didn't sleep very well. I'll be all right again after a good night's rest."

When I left the hospital I found that it was later than I thought. I had missed the bus to the village, although fortunately I would still be able to catch a bus to the end of the loch road. The village is a good four miles down the winding loch road, yet the thought of having to walk it now did not worry me. I had walked it many times before, for the buses to and from the village are few and far apart, and I had left everything ready for my father.

The loch road is single track with passing places at intervals along it. It leaves the top road with a tortuous twist. At the end of the bend is a group of cottages and a small shack that sells an assortment of groceries and sweets and cigarettes. The road widens out here for about 20 yards or so. As I came around the bend I saw a van parked there under the trees by the shack and I recognized it as belonging to Tom's father even before Tom jumped down from it.

"I've been waiting for you," he said. "Like a lift back?"

"Thanks," I said. "I would. But how did you know I'd be wanting one?"

He helped me to the seat in front and climbed into the driver's seat beside me.

"You can't do anything without everybody knowing about it," he said cheerfully. "You were seen getting on the bus. I guessed you'd gone to see Jenny and I was

138

watching for you on the bus back. That's how I knew you'd missed it."

Then his manner changed and he looked at me anxiously. "How is Jenny?"

"She's all right," I said shortly. "She'll be home in a day or two."

We sat looking at each other, then Tom looked away and started fingering the controls of the van.

"I'm glad it's nothing serious then," he said slowly. "Your father said yesterday it might be appendicitis, but today . . ."

"What did he say today?"

"He hasn't said a word all day to anyone. So I wondered . . ."

"Yes, Tom. What did you wonder?"

"Well, I wondered what was really wrong with her, that's all."

"What do *you* think is wrong with her?"

He looked at me swiftly, then looked away again. "My mother said you told them . . ."

"No matter what I told them," I interrupted, "What do *you* think is wrong, Tom?"

He turned towards me again and his face was full of worry. "Hell! She's not having a baby, is she? She told me she wasn't."

"No. She's not. But she might have,

mightn't she?"

"Yes," he said miserably. "That's what was worrying me all the time."

"It's been worrying Jenny too," I said sharply. "That's what's been wrong with her for the past weeks. Well, you were lucky this time. You got away with it. What do you think her life would be like if she *was* having a baby?"

"See here," he said, and there was a flash of anger in his eyes now. "Things are not what you seem to think they are. There won't be another time like this. Oh, I admit we were both foolish," he went on, "but don't think we haven't both regretted it ever since. I love Jenny. Really love her, I mean. I want to marry her and I'm not going to risk losing her. I know now that although she's full of fun, no matter what she says or how devil-may-care she may pretend to be, she can't get away from the way she's been brought up. She can't fly in the face of your father, nor the rest of the village either, no matter how much she'd like to. And I suppose, in spite of all my bravado, I'm much the same myself."

"Well, that's a comfort," I said.

He stared in front of him for a while, then he turned back to me. "All I want now is for Jenny to be her old self again. I want us to be what we were to each other before. She's grown away from me in the last few weeks. Don't think I haven't been miserable too."

"Well, I see no reason why she shouldn't become her old self again and you can help her probably more than anybody. She hasn't really changed towards you, Tom. Now this worry about having a baby is behind her, you'll soon find that out for yourself."

"Well, I'm certainly glad to hear you say that. If she's not happy from now on it won't be my fault."

His cheerfulness returned and with some of his old dash he started up the van and swung it back on to the road. "Better be getting you home," he said with a grin as he took the first bend at what I thought was rather a reckless speed. However, I soon saw that he was a very competent driver and relaxing back on my seat I began to enjoy the sensation of speed his driving created, for I was cheered myself to see his genuine concern for Jenny's happiness. I had always liked him and now I found myself liking him more.

"There's no one around here can touch Jenny," he said. "I still remember that first day she crossed to the island."

"She won't be crossing any more. My father doesn't want her to go back to work at the House."

He gave me a quick look of astonishment, swinging his eyes back immediately to the road ahead. "Why not? That was what he always wanted, wasn't it, to have you both over there with him? And Jenny was very happy there."

"Yes, I know. She'll need to take things a bit easier for a while though. She may be able to find something a little less tiring in the village."

"What does Jenny think about it?"

"Oh, I think she'll be quite content to change."

"Well, so long as he's not pushing her into it against her will," he said doubtfully. "Your father's not exactly easy-going, is he? What upset him today?"

"Oh, we had a bit of a quarrel," I said shortly, not wanting him to pursue that subject. Jenny could tell Tom what she liked, but at the moment I preferred to keep him in ignorance of the true situation.

As I thanked him for the lift home he said, "I'm glad we had this chance to talk. I feel so much happier about Jenny now, for one thing. I was pretty worried about her before, especially after seeing your father today." He gave me a cheeky grin. "You know, I've always been a bit scared of my future father-in-law and a bit in awe of my future sister-in-law. I couldn't say I'm quite happy about my father-in-law yet, but I think I'm going to enjoy having you as a sister-in-law."

Chapter Ten

IT seemed strange crossing to the island without Jenny. I had been so happy in the pattern that my life had lately taken on and now, suddenly, everything was changing. Even in the village, where I had thought life passed us by, we had the same problems to face that people everywhere have. Human nature is very little changed by either time or place.

Meg questioned me more closely than anyone else, for she had been so concerned about Jenny. I knew my answers failed to satisfy her and she could see no reason why Jenny should not come back to the House once she was well again.

"I miss her so much," she kept telling me. "It's not half as much fun here without her. She likes it here and the work *isn't* too hard. Can't you put that silly idea out of your father's head?"

I couldn't tell her that, knowing what my father believed, I too thought it was better for her not to come back to the island. I disliked the half-truths I was constantly telling and the evasive answers I gave, but it seemed to me it was all for the best.

Mrs Willis was completely taken aback when I told her that Jenny would not be coming across any more.

"I thought she was very happy here."

"Oh, she was," I said hastily. "She's always liked working here. But my father thinks she might be better off now with a different kind of job."

She gave me a curious look and for a moment she didn't say anything. Then she said, "Well, she was a good girl and I'll be sorry to lose her. But if that's what your father thinks, I suppose there's nothing more to be said about it."

It was with a strange mixture of feelings that I opened the door to my little office. The connecting door to Mark Sutherby's

144

room was open and he was already in there. He heard me come in and he came to the doorway as I was hanging my jacket on the peg. His smile of welcome brought a lump to my throat, making me realise what a keyed-up state I was in.

"I've missed you," he said. "I'm glad you're back."

He spoke sincerely as if he meant what he said and was not just offering a polite greeting. I would have taken pleasure from his remark before, but now I felt a little stab of pain.

"I was sorry to hear about your sister," he said as I followed him into his room. "How is she getting on?"

"Very well. She'll be home in a day or two."

"So it's nothing serious. I'm glad of that. Nobody seemed to know just exactly what was wrong. Your father was no help at all."

I looked at him quickly. "You've spoken to him?"

"I tried. He's about as talkative as a mute. But then, he never has been exactly brimming over with cordiality towards me." He gave a little wry smile. "I don't think he's ever quite got over that day in the garden."

145

I took a deep breath of relief. So my father had kept his suspicions to himself. For what reason, I couldn't guess, unless I had left a doubt in his mind after all. I hoped now that he would keep quiet until Jenny found the courage to tell him the truth.

I could feel him looking at me. "You've been overdoing things, haven't you? Perhaps you shouldn't have come across today."

"I'm all right," I said. "A little tired, that's all." To stop any more questions I began to talk about his work.

"I haven't done much while you've been away. I couldn't settle down to it the same. I told you you'd become indispensable to me, didn't I?"

Again I felt a dart of pain. I felt I should warn him that I would soon be leaving him but I couldn't bring myself to do so just then.

We worked together for the rest of the morning and already I knew that things would never be quite the same between us again. I had been natural and unselfconscious with him before but now I weighed every word I said and I knew my manner was constrained, yet I could not help it. By lunch time I felt miserable and

146

he too had fallen silent.

After lunch I stayed talking to Mrs Willis longer than usual and then found Meg. I wanted no intimate walk or talk today for I was so afraid of giving myself away.

When I went back in he was already at his desk and he watched me with a serious, brooding expression on his face as I walked over to join him. I did my best to behave as if everything was normal but I knew that the strained atmosphere of the morning was still there.

Presently he laid down his papers and looked at me. "There's something wrong, isn't there? Is it Jenny?"

I shook my head, not knowing how to answer.

"I don't want to pry," he said, "but you must know that if there's any way I can help you I would. Would it help you to talk about it?"

"I'm really just tired," I insisted. "I *was* worried about Jenny at first. But I know she's all right now."

He didn't press me any further and went back to his work. Still I said nothing to him about leaving, but the day had convinced me more than ever that I must go as soon as possible.

Even so I knew I couldn't go until I was assured that Jenny's life, when she came home from the hospital, would not be one of misery. At the moment it seemed apparent that it would be. My father scarcely spoke and the atmosphere at home was such as to make the most cheerful person depressed. I felt I couldn't stand it for long myself and I couldn't go and abandon Jenny to it at such a time, for her homecoming was hardly likely to improve matters.

I took some sewing into the living room that evening and sat turning things over in my mind. My father was painting a cupboard out in the kitchen and I was glad that I was alone for my mind was so pre-occupied that for most of the time I sat staring into space, my sewing forgotten.

It seemed that my father was the only stumbling-block in the way of Jenny's happiness and my freedom to leave home. With this in mind I decided to speak to him. When I went into the kitchen he had just finished painting and was cleaning his brushes.

"Father, I've been thinking things over. I want to change my job as soon as possible."

"Well, I'm glad to hear you've come to your senses at last," he said slowly, without turning round or stopping his brush-cleaning.

"You realise that I won't be able to come home every day."

He turned and looked at me then. "So now you want to leave home," he said with bitterness in his voice.

"There's no alternative, Father, if I'm to leave the House. There's nothing for me in the village."

He stood looking at me. "All right," he said at last. "Go and get your job in the town. The sooner you leave this one the easier I'll be in my mind." He turned back to the sink.

"Jenny will be home soon," I said. "I'll not go until I see her settled down and happy again."

"That's your affair," he said curtly.

"No, Father. It's your affair, as you know very well."

He turned round angrily, his brush dripping on the floor unheeded. "What are you trying to tell me?"

"You can make Jenny's life happy or you can make it miserable."

"Jenny made her own bed. Let her lie on it."

"Jenny can't undo the past. Nor is she

149

likely to forget it. But she can make a future for herself if you'll let her."

"What sort of future do you think she's got now?" he said scornfully.

"Why don't you let Jenny work that out for herself? At least don't make it more difficult for her. What good will it do you, Father, or anyone else, to live with the past at your elbow all the time."

"Some things will not be forgotten so easily as you seem to think," he said bitterly. "I had a daughter who was good and innocent. What is she now?"

"She's still your daughter. Can't you see that she wants to get back where she was. Will you be the one to refuse her help?"

"You stand there preaching at me. Are you such a paragon yourself?"

"None of us is perfect, Father, and I've never imagined that I am. I want to forget the past, too, and start again. You can help us both."

He said no more then nor for the rest of the evening, but from then on the tension between us was eased a little and he gradually became less frigid and unapproachable in his attitude towards me.

Jenny came home a few days later. I had intended to go in on the bus to bring her home but Tom asked me if he could drive me in and bring us both back. If I could go in the afternoon he could pick up some supplies in Tollie at the same time. I accepted his offer gladly for I thought that if Tom were there to meet her it would be a happy start for her for I knew she was dreading her homecoming.

She was ready for me when I arrived and she seemed quite calm and self-possessed, at least on the surface. She was still pale though and quite a bit thinner. She had changed in a more subtle way too and she seemed older and more sedate.

She was delighted to see Tom and the three of us squeezed up on the front seat of the van with Jenny in the middle. She didn't talk much on the way home and there was no sign of her old bubbling spirits. But there was no doubt that both she and Tom were happy to be in each other's company again. There was certainly no tension there now.

My father came in soon after we arrived home. As we heard his key in the lock we both stopped talking and I doubt if Jenny was more nervous of her reception than I was. He came into the room and stood looking at her and for a moment nobody spoke.

Then Jenny's calm deserted her. Suddenly she ran to him, flinging her arms around him as if she were a little girl again. "Father," was all she could say before she burst into tears.

My father looked slightly bewildered and slowly he raised his hand and stroked her hair as if she really were once again his little girl. His eyes met mine over the top of her head and I turned away. I knew that he was struggling between his wish to comfort her and his sense of duty to deal sternly with her.

"There's lots I should be saying to you," he said at last, "and doubtless you know what I've been thinking and feeling. But I'll say no more than this now. You've done something you can't forget, lass. Something that will be with you always. Something that some day will come between you and the man you want to marry. For if such a day should come you'll have no right to hide it from him."

Jenny fumbled for her handkerchief and checked her sobs. When she was quiet she said in a small voice, "That day will come, Father, for that's what I want. And this will be no secret between us I can promise you."

I left them together and went into the

kitchen, filled with relief. Without premeditation or conscious effort, Jenny, by her behaviour, had broken down the first painful barrier between them.

As the days went by it seemed that they might learn to live in harmony together more quickly than I had thought, for the change in Jenny was even more apparent now. She was very much quieter and more content to be quiet and in her very quietness there seemed a new strength as if at last she knew where she was going and was content to bide her time.

My father was not slow to notice the change either and his first close watchfulness of her began to relax. His mood was lighter too and in spite of all that had happened we were beginning to draw together again.

Jenny found herself a job in the village drapery shop, a dingy little place owned by an elderly spinster, Miss Lang. She wouldn't have stuck it for one week in the old days but now she went along uncomplainingly and even managed to stay cheerful too. In one way the change of job turned out for the better after all for she told me that she and Tom found opportunities of meeting during the day which they hadn't had before.

My own composure returned to me as I watched Jenny settle down, but even so my days on the island were still a great strain. There was a tension now between us that I seemed unable to ease. He no longer played his records and now we didn't talk to each other except about the work. Sometimes I could feel him watching me and if I caught his glance I saw a look of sadness in his eyes that I never tried to explain for it disturbed me so deeply that I became panicky and made some foolish remark, trying to appear light-hearted.

After my first deliberate avoidance of him in the lunch hour he had stopped seeking me out and so I was surprised one day to come out and find him waiting for me.

"Let us walk across the island," he said shortly, more like an order than an invitation, and giving me no time to answer he turned and walked off. After a second of hesitation I followed him.

We walked in silence for he seemed very lost in his thoughts, his face serious as he looked ahead. When we came out on the beach on the far side he stopped and turned towards me and his eyes as they looked at me were so intense, so searching, that I felt the blood hot in my face. My heart beat rapidly and to ease the tension in me and cover my confusion I moved over and sat down on the rocks where we'd sat before on our previous walks. He followed me but he did not sit down. Instead he stood directly in front of me, looking down on me with that strange, sharpened look.

"What has happened, Ann? Why have you changed towards me?"

He spoke and acted almost as if there was some intimate relationship between us, and it sent a wild thrill through me. I looked up at him, trying to read in his face some of the feeling for me that I felt for him. The wide, tawny eyes told me nothing. Only the way he stood over me kept the feeling of intimacy between us.

I looked down from his unwavering gaze, fearful of giving myself away. What if he did feel an attraction for me, wildly unlikely as it seemed. He already had a wife and to me with my strict code of morals so firmly implanted by my upbringing, love was forbidden where marriage was not possible.

"You must tell me," he insisted, "what I have done to offend you. It is important that I know. Important to me, that is."

I looked at him, swiftly denying his words.

"You've done nothing to offend me."

"You can't deny that you've changed towards me, avoiding me where once you were happy to be in my company, or so I thought. Is it something I've said or done? At least give me the chance to explain it away."

"There's nothing to explain away," I said desperately, getting to my feet and escaping past him.

We stood a few feet apart looking at each other and he made no attempt now to come closer. His face was shadowed and full of a pain which I was too disturbed to try to explain. Then slowly the old mask of bitterness came down over it and the expressive eyes were hidden under the drawn-down brows. He gave a short laugh which had nothing of humour in it.

"I must be the world's biggest fool," he said. Then he turned abruptly away and walked down to the water's edge.

I stood watching him. His hands were in his pockets and his shoulders hunched. It was a typical attitude of his when he was upset or dejected as I had come to know. I could see only the profile of his still face but I knew that he was desperately unhappy. I didn't understand why for I couldn't believe that my avoidance of him could be the cause. I longed to go to him, to comfort him and be comforted by him. Suddenly I was filled with an angry resentment. Why was he denied to me? Why was Fiona there between us? She couldn't really love him to abandon him as she had. I would never leave him if I were married to him.

Hot tears pricked my eyelids and impatiently I brushed them away. What kind of fool was I to picture myself in Fiona's place? Fiona of wealthy family, beautiful and elegant; all the things that I was not. She belonged to Mark's world. She belonged to Mark as I never could. What interest could he have in me beyond the fact that I helped him in his writing. If he was worried about offending me it was only that he feared I might leave him before the book was finished.

I left the beach and walked swiftly back to the house and as I walked I knew that I must tell him now that I was going.

Chapter Eleven

I WAS in my own room finishing the typing

of a completed chapter when I heard Mark come back into his study. My hands were shaking as I collected the sheets to take into him for I intended to tell him now that I was leaving him.

"Ah, another chapter finished," he said as I came in. "This book's going to be finished sooner than I thought, thanks largely to your help. I've got another one fairly well planned. We'll be starting on that before the end of the summer at this rate."

His face now was expressionless but his eyes watched me closely. I suspected that he guessed what was in my mind and had spoken as he had deliberately in order to find out.

"I won't be with you for that," I said quietly, trying to keep the tremble out of my voice.

I watched his face harden and there was bitterness in his voice when he spoke again.

"So you're deserting me."

"I told you when I first came that I wouldn't be staying for long," I said, hoping that he would accept this for explanation.

He was silent, looking down on his hands that were clasped before him on the desk.

"When are you thinking of leaving?" he

158

asked at last without looking up.

"As soon as possible."

He looked up then and again I saw that look of pain in his eyes that I'd seen on the beach. He looked lost and hurt, like an abandoned child. Was it all because of my going? As I looked at him sitting there he seemed again the lonely person that I'd thought him when I first came to the island. Perhaps even my companionship had meant something to him. Again I wanted to comfort him.

"You'll find somebody else. I'll wait until then if you want me to."

"Where will I find another like you?" he said. "Tell me that."

The gentleness in his voice and the way he was looking at me now loosed a wild rush of emotion in me. I could no longer meet his eyes and I turned away, nervously fingering the papers I still held. He pushed back his chair and walked over to the window, standing with his back to me.

"Perhaps it's better this way," he said after a while, "for how else could it end?"

I stood there uncertainly with nothing to say, still not understanding him.

He made no move and presently I placed the typed sheets on the desk for him, thinking to go back to my room. He turned then and came back to the desk and with a swift movement swept all his papers into a pile.

"That's the end of that," he said. "I'll not be doing any more to the book."

I stared in dismay at the untidy pile that had been so carefully sifted and selected.

"You can't give it up now. You're nearly through it."

He stared back at me, leaning on the desk. "Why should you care? What do you care about the book, or me?"

I couldn't bear that he should think this. "I do care," I said with some passion. "Both about the book and you."

Slowly he straightened up, still looking at me. "Then you have a very strange way of showing it," he said quietly.

He came round from behind the desk and stood close to me. "Do you care, Ann? Do you?"

I looked into his eyes, wide open and soft, almost pleading it seemed, and I longed to tell him how much I really cared.

"Why are you leaving me, Ann?"

"I just want to leave the village, I always have," I said desperately.

"But now it's because you want to leave

me." There was sadness in his face and in his voice.

He turned away and began to pace the room, then suddenly he came swiftly back to me. "The truth, Ann. You must tell me the truth. Why are you running away? Do you think that I'm in love with you and you find the idea repelling?" His eyes burned with a strange light as they watched my face.

"No, oh no," I said, appalled that he should think such a thing.

"Well, I do love you," he said more quietly. "Haven't you guessed?"

I could only stare at him, unable yet to realise the full meaning of what he was saying.

"Tell me now, before you go. If I had been free to offer you my love, do you think you could ever have come to love me in return?"

My voice was no more than a whisper, sticking in my throat. "I do love you."

For a moment he looked at me almost in disbelief, then his face lit up and his eyes shone more brilliantly than I'd ever seen them.

"Oh my dear, say that again. I can't believe that I heard you right."

"I love you already," I said, still in a whisper, for I was so overwhelmed by my own feelings that I couldn't control my voice.

Then I was in his arms, my head pressed against his shoulder as he held me close. I could feel the beat of his heart and the warmth of his body; the strength of his arms as they held me tight against him. He loved me. The knowledge filled me with exaltation, yet with it was a stillness and quiet of indescribable sweetness so that I scarcely dared breathe for fear of breaking its magic.

I had forgotten Fiona. Now there was no past and no future; only the present where my happiness was so great there was no room for anything else.

Presently he pushed me gently from him and looked down into my face with a little frown. "Do you really love me, Ann, or did I push you into saying more than you really meant. Perhaps you will regret what you said when you've had time to think things over."

"Oh, no," I said swiftly. "I do love you, truly love you. I knew it before today. That's why I was leaving you."

"Why did you think you had to leave me? Because you thought I didn't love you or because of my being married?"

"Both," I said, and now the pain was back as I was reminded of Fiona. "Oh, Mark, it's no use, is it?"

He pulled me to him again. "It's you I love, and only you. You must believe that," he said, almost fiercely. "Nor are we harming Fiona. Everything was over between us years ago. You must believe that too."

I looked up into his face and I knew that he was speaking the truth.

His hand caressed my hair but his eyes were troubled as they looked beyond me. "In this moment of knowing you love me my happiness is complete. Yet how can it last, for I still have no right to your love."

I reached up my hand to smooth away the worried lines in his face. "Nothing can destroy my happiness in knowing that you love me."

He smiled then and bent his head to kiss me. "Nor mine in knowing that you love me. Oh, my dearest, if only we could have met at the beginning. But I was born too soon or you too late. The past has happened and there's no undoing it. You are so young, so unspoiled. You deserve the love of someone other than me . . ."

"It's your love I want," I said, stopping him. "I shall never want anyone else."

"Do you realize I'm already thirty-nine?"

"And I'm already twenty-six. I don't feel there's much difference between us." ∧

"Perhaps you're right. What difference do years make? Before I met you I felt that I'd lived forever. Now I'm as young as you. What does it matter how far we've come. Now we are as one and are ageless to each other."

Again he kissed me. "You have that look in your eyes that I wanted so much to see there. Let me keep it there, at least for today. There's a lot I ought to tell you, but it can keep until tomorrow."

With his arm around me he led me across to the long settee and drew me down to sit beside him.

"These last few days I've been in torment," he said, "wondering what had turned you against me. Now I am at peace. Peace and happiness, you've brought me both, when I never expected to find either of them again."

He sat considering me with a serious expression. "You've never been anything but good for me. Whenever I look into those clear grey eyes I see the image of what

I ought to be, what I once was. When I'm with you I'm myself again and the past is wiped out."

He took my hands, pressing them in his. "Oh, my darling, with you I could be so happy. If only I could keep you with me I would ask for nothing else."

"But we can't belong to each other. That's what you're telling me, isn't it?"

Again I felt the pain and sadness, for although for a while the miracle of his love for me had made almost anything seem possible, I had never really believed that we could.

Letting go of my hands he stood up and began restlessly to walk about. After a while he came back and stood in front of me. "I told you that everything is over between Fiona and me, and that of course is true. But I'm still not free to do as I want. I won't be free till Peter's through University and ready to come here and take up his inheritance. How can I expect you to wait that long? You're so young still, and you have your own life to lead."

He dropped to the floor beside me and with his arm around my waist buried his head in my lap. "Oh, Ann, must I lose you just as I've found you?"

I smoothed his bright hair, feeling again almost as if I were comforting a child. "If we're to lose each other it will not be through my doing. Without you I shall never be truly happy again."

He stayed there still and silent.

"Do you mean that the House and the island will belong to Peter then and not to you?" I asked presently, thinking over his words.

He lifted his head and gave me an odd little smile. "Yes, they were left to him by his grandfather. I am only here until he is ready to step into his grandfather's shoes. If you decide to wait for me I shall take you far from your home, for this place will never be *my* home. Does that worry you?"

"Nothing worries me except the thought of being separated from you. I'll wait as long as I have to and go to the ends of the earth if necessary."

He got up from the floor and sitting down beside me drew me into his arms. "When I'm free of the island, Fiona and I can be free of each other too, which is what we both want. Then at last I'll be able to ask you to marry me. Will you really wait that long for me?"

"You are offering me more happiness

166

than I ever dreamed of. Of course I'll wait," I said.

We sat there together for a long time, sometimes talking, sometimes silent, until at last I realised how late it must be getting. I had been so completely lost in my new happiness I seemed to have moved into another world. I looked at the time and sat up suddenly.

"I must go or they'll be waiting for me."

Mark stood up, pulling me to my feet. "We mustn't have your father coming to look for you. I'm afraid he dislikes me enough as it is. In fact," he went on, suddenly serious, "history seems to be repeating itself." He looked at me strangely and his face became shadowed. "But it couldn't. Not beyond that fact. Not with you, Ann."

"What do you mean, Mark?" I asked, puzzled by his words and his change of manner.

He didn't answer directly. "Nothing can take today from men, anyway," he said, "because it's already happened."

Meg was still waiting for me at the back of the house. "We'll have to run for it," she said as soon as I appeared. "You're very late and they'll be getting impatient."

I was glad that our hurry made it impossible for any gossip between us and as we ran down to the boat I tried to push myself back into my everyday life. It was difficult to behave as if all was as usual for at times during the evening it seemed I must explode with the happiness inside me. But I knew that I could not tell my father yet what had happened that afternoon. Not to Jenny either would I give any hint as to how things stood between Mark and myself.

It was a relief to get to bed where, my face hidden, I could at last let my thoughts turn where they wanted. I seemed now to be a different person from what I had been before, as if my true self was only just beginning to wake up. Life had suddenly taken on a new depth, a new richness and I was eager to live it to the full. I knew now it could only be complete with Mark. I knew too that we could belong to each other, that all the gulfs I'd thought existed between us were no longer there. It was true that Mark, for some strange reason, was still tied to Fiona. But they didn't love each other. Mark loved me and wanted to marry me. There was no cloud to spoil my happiness, a happiness which only that morning I had thought impossible.

Chapter Twelve

WHEN I woke next morning I could hear the rain beating against the window-pane and a gusty wind tugged at the loose frame. When I looked out across the loch the island was invisible, hidden by driving sheets of rain. It was a day typical of so many, when the rain never ceases and the wind is chilly. A day when the fires would be lit over in the House even though we were into summer.

"Listen to that rain," Jenny said as we were getting ready. "I'm not sorry to be missing the boat journey today."

It was the first time she had made any reference to her old job, even indirectly, and I looked at her curiously, wondering how much she missed Meg's cheerful company for the two of them had made light of their work together.

"How's it going at the shop?" I asked. "Do you find it very dull?"

"It would be impossibly so without something to look forward to," she said quietly. "But I see Tom every day and I'm content to wait."

There was a calm serenity in her face and again I thought how mature she had become, closing the gap the difference in our ages had once made between us. I felt a new rush of warmth for her for now I understood her completely. There was nothing but good in her and she deserved her happiness. It seemed that I too must be content to wait, perhaps longer than Jenny.

Mark was waiting for me when I reached my room and when I'd removed my dripping mac and scarf he took me across to the fire that burned in the huge fireplace of his study, just as I had pictured it when looking across the loch.

"What a day to be crossing in that boat," he said. "This loch can be pretty treacherous from what I've heard. Are you never afraid?"

I shook my head, shaking the loose rain-drops from the front of my hair at the same time. Laughingly he produced a handkerchief from his pocket.

"Let me dry you off. The rain's running down your face like tears. You've rain-drops on your eye-lashes too. They give those grey eyes of yours a misty look which is most attractive. You have very beautiful eyes, Ann. I find everything about you beautiful."

He took me into his arms and kissed me. "I was so afraid you might disappear overnight, or change your mind. Do you still feel as you did yesterday?"

"I shall never change," I told him.

He gave me a long look, then turning to the fire he poked it with the toe of his shoe, making the coals burst into new flame and sparks fly up the chimney. He pulled the couch towards the fire and drew me down to sit beside him.

"Yesterday was ours," he said. "Ours alone. I wanted to keep it that way. All the same there are things you should know, things that concern *you* now. You must have wondered, for instance, why Fiona and I were not divorced long ago. Well, there are no principles involved, no religious objections. We are tied together by my dear dead father-in-law, to be separated only when Peter mounts the vacated throne here."

I could only stare at him in astonishment.

"You may well look surprised. I told you once, if you remember, that you didn't know the half of it. To explain it all to you I must go back a long way. It isn't a pretty story and I'll be as brief as I can."

He got up and went and stood with his back to the fireplace and as he talked I watched him withdraw into the past. His eyes stared ahead, seeing only the pictures his memory conjured up. His face was shadowed and his voice grew more and more bitter as he went on.

Through his words I too went back with him, back to his last weeks at University when he first met Fiona while she was staying with her friends down in England. I saw him returning from the island, spurned and insulted by Fiona's father, the first seeds of his hatred for his father-in-law sown in him. I imagined Fiona, driven from home by her father's pressures upon her, turning up at the tiny flatlet in London he could barely afford as a young man just starting out to earn his living. And I pictured the hasty marriage, entered into with such high hopes.

"We were happy enough at first," Mark said, "but Fiona soon grew restless and irritable under the restrictions our lack of money put upon her. I had warned her that we would only have my small salary to live on but she really had no idea of the value of money and I couldn't blame her for that. To make matters worse she was very soon pregnant. Inevitably we quarrelled. All marriages have their quarrels I suppose, but ours were so bitter. We were soon too far away from each other ever to get back."

The hurt of those days showed in his face and I wanted to put my arms around him and tell him that it was all over now. But I sat still and quiet. I guessed that none of it had ever been told to anyone. Perhaps he would find some ease now in opening up the dark places in his mind instead of brooding over them himself.

"When Peter was born things went from bad to worse," he said. "Fiona lost interest in everything, including herself. She seemed to have no strength, no will to do anything. I was appalled at what our marriage had done to her in so short a time. I was filled with guilt too at my irresponsibility in rushing so blindly into it and of having a child so soon.

"Within a few weeks of Peter's birth Fiona's father paid us a visit. It was the first she'd seen or heard of him since she'd left home, but I found out later that he'd kept track of us all the time and that the timing of his visit now was no accident. He came during the day and I didn't see him. When I came home Fiona was a different person and her listlessness was gone."

Mark paused and there was a long silence. He seemed so far away from me that I began to wonder if he'd forgotten I was there. He took a few turns around the room while I sat and watched him. Then he came back and stood in front of me.

"Duncan offered a solution to our problems, Ann. He would take Fiona out of her miserable existence in the flat, set her up in a fine house and give her a handsome allowance. Of course there were conditions, two to be exact. One was that Peter was to be brought up as *he* wished with the object of eventually making him his heir. He was to live in Fiona's fine house until he was old enough to go away to school. Then he was to spend all his holidays on the island with his grandfather."

"I see," I said, beginning now to understand some of the things that had puzzled me, especially where Peter was concerned. "And what was the other condition?"

"That neither Fiona nor I would seek a divorce before Peter was twenty-one years old."

"Why on earth should he insist on that? I mean, it doesn't make sense, does it? I thought you said that he offered the house to Fiona only. Surely he was encouraging her to separate from you."

"Oh, he didn't care whether we separated or not. He knew our marriage was on the rocks either way. He just didn't want either of us to have a second chance at marriage, not whilst we had our youth anyway. We had married each other against his wishes; hit him where it hurt most, in his pride. He was not the man to forget that. Besides, I think it went even deeper than that. He would never forgive me for marrying his daughter, that I might understand, but now he hated me for having the son that was denied to him. He wanted to take that son from me and at the same time deny me the chance of having another. He was pretty safe in assuming that Fiona would never have another child of mine, divorce or no divorce."

"Mark, that's monstrous. I can't believe it."

He gave me a bleak little smile. "He practically admitted as much to Fiona. It's difficult to believe that anyone could be so vindictive, I know."

He walked across to the window and stood with his back to me staring out at the driving rain. "It's even more difficult to believe that anyone would let him get away with it," he said with sudden violence. "Why did I do it? Oh, Ann, why did I do it? That question has tortured me."

"Why *did* you agree to it, Mark? Surely there must have been some other way out."

"I couldn't see any other. And Fiona wanted it that way. It meant a new life for her."

"Was money that important to her?"

"What else did she have. With me there was nothing."

"She had her child. And she had your love."

"No. She didn't have my love. Not any longer. And this only added to my feeling of guilt at the life she was leading. Oh, I loved her all right when I married her. Or rather I thought I did. But I didn't really know what true love was then."

"She couldn't really have loved you, either, could she?"

He shrugged and made no answer to this. He was silent for a long time, staring out through the window, and I guessed he was remembering all the arguments that must have taken place between the two of them before he would agree to her father's proposal. Presently he gave a long sigh and then came and stood behind me so that I couldn't see him without moving.

"Well, I gave in, Ann. I did what Fiona wanted. You may call it weakness, or

cowardice; perhaps selfishness or an obsession of guilt. No matter what you call it, is
there anything that can justify my
behaviour? Somehow I persuaded myself
that there was. Was I right, Ann? I've told
you the circumstances. What should I have
done?"

How could I judge him, seeing things as I
did only through my own eyes? How could I
really put myself in his place?

"Duncan Reddie was an evil man," I
said, not answering his question. "I thought
he was austere and hard, but I didn't realise
he was so full of evil."

"He was held in high regard here. They
all say he was a good master. He was a good
father until Fiona set him against her. He
was good to Peter too, the boy was really
fond of him. But he was a man with an
obsession; an obsession that dominated his
life and made him act the way he did. All
the while Fiona's mother was alive he was
obsessed by the fact that she had not given
him a son. He wanted an heir more than
anything. Someone to carry on the family
name, to go on building the family fortunes.
When he saw that he was not to have his
son he pinned his hopes on Fiona marrying
that young cousin of his. The name would

still be here and they would most likely have a son to follow on. That hope too was dashed when she ran off and married me."

"He could have married again himself and maybe had the heir he wanted."

"Yes, he could have, and I don't know why he didn't. Perhaps he would have if Peter had not been born, who knows? But Peter was born so soon, while he was still sitting here boiling with rage and frustration no doubt. Perhaps his desire for revenge was as great then as his need for an heir. Peter was the answer to both."

I sat staring into the fire, thinking over all that Mark had told me.

"Now you know, Ann, why I'm not free to marry you yet, though, God knows, I'd give almost anything to be able to. You also know now more about the kind of person I am."

The wind was noisy in the chimney and I didn't hear his footsteps on the carpet. Only when he spoke from the doorway did I realise that he'd moved away from behind me.

"I promised to go and see Martin this morning. He's got some scheme afoot which he says I must approve before he can go ahead. Merely a gesture really. He knows as well as I do that I know very little about these things, but there it is. Perhaps by the time I come back you will not feel the same towards me. I should have told you everything before I let you make all those promises. But I'll not hold you to them if you want to change your mind."

Before I could answer him he was gone.

Chapter Thirteen

WHEN Mark left me I sat on by the fireside thinking over what he had told me. Now I understood his dislike of the island and of everything to do with Duncan Reddie, his strange attitude towards Peter. And I could understand too how he had become the touchy person I had first known.

And I could see how I had come to love him. His younger self was not dead, only buried. Pushed away in order not to be hurt more. I had seen glimpses of it almost from the beginning and the longer I knew him the more I had come to know his true self. Now, if anything, I loved him more, not less, as he seemed to fear. I told myself that never again would he know the unhappiness of the past for I loved and needed him just as he loved and needed me.

I thought about the life he had shared with Fiona, so different from what I had always imagined. I had been so envious of her but I need never be so again. His love for her had been so brief, perhaps no more than a youthful attraction mistaken for love. And she didn't love him. Although I had suspected this I was glad to know it was true. She would not stand between us.

He was not back by the end of the morning and I was still day-dreaming when I went along for my lunch. As I sat opposite Mrs Willis I wondered if she knew or guessed at the situation between Mark and Fiona. If she did she had never hinted at it. I hoped she would not guess at the situation between Mark and myself for it would be a long time, it seemed, before we could bring it into the open.

When I went back to the study he was already there, standing in front of the fire. He watched me as I crossed the room towards him and he put an arm around my shoulders as I stood near him. "I'm sorry, I was away longer than I expected. Still, it's given you plenty of time to think about things. Your face tells me that you haven't changed towards me."

I smiled up at him. "Everything I said still stands. And now I know that some day we can belong to each other, which is more than I thought possible once."

"You haven't passed judgment on me yet. You haven't said what I should or should not have done."

"Mark," I said, considering this, "you love Peter don't you? I've seen it only too plainly for myself. But it isn't just that. You want *his* love too, you want his respect. This is not a new thing is it? Haven't you always felt that way?"

"Yes, I've always felt that way. I had a normal father's pride in a new-born son. I hated the thought of parting from him. The farther away from me he became the more I wanted him."

"Then were you never tempted to do something about it? I mean, even though you'd given in in the first place, as time went by . . ."

He took me up as I hesitated. "Yes, as time went by I was frequently tempted, especially in those early years before he went away to school. But we'd only have been back where we started then. Fiona would have been thrown back on me for there was no one else she could turn to. She would have hated me for it. Besides, as Peter grew older he seemed to sense the atmosphere between us. He was all right with Fiona alone or with me alone but obviously unhappy if the three of us were together."

"You were able to see him then?"

"Oh yes, quite frequently when he was young. Duncan made no condition there. Perhaps he knew I'd feel worse the more I saw of him, it would be like him to think of that. We even kept up a pretence that it was my work that kept me away from home. Once he went away to school I saw very little of him. Then I found that he was nervous with me and rather afraid of me too, and no wonder. I always managed to snap and snarl around him, though it was really the last thing I wanted to do. It infuriated me to hear him talk about his grandfather so much and to watch his growing admiration and affection for him. Besides, I'd become such a bitter, unreasonable person by then. I quarrelled with everyone."

"What about now, Mark?" I said presently. "Duncan's dead. Can you and Fiona not get your divorce?"

"Only by losing Peter his inheritance. It's in the will, Ann. Everything's in the will. Duncan may be dead but he's not finished with us yet."

He gave a bitter little laugh. "Of course, I haven't told you this. When Duncan found out that he hadn't long to live he got in touch with me for the one and only time. How much he'd been in touch with Fiona I never tried to find out. He told me the conditions of the will, one of which was that I was to take his place here on the island until Peter was ready to. His arrogance was typical. He knew I'd be useless here, but Martin would carry all the weight. He wanted Peter to see me in his place and compare the two of us."

"Oh, Mark, he *was* evil," I said. "No matter what everybody here seems to think of him."

"He was so sure of himself, he always was. He knew that I'd come, and he thought that I'd never change from the kind of person I'd become. The more Peter saw of me the less he would think of me."

"Well, if he could see the two of you together now he would turn in his grave. Things haven't turned out as he expected, have they?"

He hugged me to him, smiling happily again. "Ah, but what he didn't know was that when the old ogre died a good fairy would come to the island and put a very different spell on me."

I watched him as he bent to put more coal on the fire which had burned low and as he turned towards me smiling and happy I thought that he couldn't be very much different now from the young Mark who had come to the island looking for Fiona, only now he was more mature and, to me, more attractive.

"We're finished with the past," he said, "and it's best forgotten, but I wanted you to know everything. And now, what about the future? We've three long years to wait before we can think about marrying. Unless," he added, looking at me seriously, "you think I should now break my obligations."

"Oh, no," I said quickly. "I wouldn't want that. When we marry I don't want anything to spoil it."

I could see the relief in his face. "I'm so glad to hear you say that for I don't believe I could bring myself to do it. I couldn't bear to take so much from Peter now after all that's happened. But it's so long to ask you to wait. Three years of your youth gone, and I'll be well into my forties by then too."

"Oh, Mark, what does it matter? What do I care when we marry? It's enough to know that you love me. It's all I want and far more than I'd ever hoped for."

He held me close and kissed me and then we sat side by side watching the new flames licking the coals. "When you're with me I can forget all my doubts and fears," he said. "I can believe anything. I can even believe in a future of happiness together."

Presently he turned towards me and looking at me seriously said, "All right. We've decided we'll wait. Now we have to decide what we're going to do while we're waiting."

I looked at him in surprise, not knowing quite what he meant.

"You haven't had time yet to give the matter much thought. You've only just become aware of all the circumstances. But I've had time to think it all out."

He considered me with a little frown for a moment or two, then he said, "You've always wanted to get away from the island and the village, see something of the world. Now's the time."

"Oh no, not now. Things are different

now."

"Yes, things *are* different. Which is exactly why you must go."

I shook my head slowly, refusing to look at the idea. He took my hands in his and turned me towards him. "All right, Ann. What do you suggest we do? Do you want us to tell everyone we're in love, that we're going to wait for my divorce and then get married?"

"I can't tell my father, not if I'm to continue to live at home."

"And I don't want to tell Peter. He knows nothing of what I've told you. I'd rather he didn't know yet the circumstances under which I'm here. Some day I'll try to explain myself to him – I owe him that explanation – but that day's a long way off yet."

"Oh yes, Mark. You're right. It wouldn't be fair to tell him now. It would only distress him."

"What else then? Do we carry on as usual, pretending that nothing has changed – hiding our love from everybody? Do you think we could be close to each other for that long without giving ourselves away? I want no scandal for you, Ann. Nor do I want lies or deceit – a furtive kiss when no

186

one is looking. These are not for you, Ann. I respect you too much, as well as love you."

There was no answer to his argument for all he said was true. Besides, I'd already told my father that I'd soon be leaving. If I stayed on now it wouldn't be long before he wanted to know the reason why.

"We haven't much choice, my dear," Mark said gently. "We might as well face it. Whatever we do, the next three years will not be easy for either of us."

"Oh, Mark," I said miserably. "Three long years away from you."

"It needn't be a complete separation. In fact I don't see why it should be. There's no reason why I shouldn't come to see you."

I was silent, turning things over in my mind.

"Oh, Ann," he said, gripping my hands more tightly. "If we were in London or some other large city where nobody cared what we did I might be selfish and persuade you to stay close to me, for I dread the separation even more than you do. But here! In this place! In this house! Think of the passion and the prejudices we'd arouse. The very ghosts would rise out of that burial ground to torment us. We must wait until

I'm free to marry you and take you away. Then it won't matter what anybody says or thinks."

Still I was silent and after a while he got up and went to stand again in front of the fireplace. "There's another thing too," he said. "I'm old enough to know that I truly love you, in every sense of the word. Old enough to know that nothing can change that love. By the end of the three years I shall only want you more, if that is possible. But you're still young, my dear. You've been shut away in this remote place all your life. You've met scarcely anyone. When you're let loose in the world outside you may well find someone who attracts you more."

"Mark! How can you say that? How can you doubt me?"

"I don't doubt your love for me now, much as I marvel at it. And if you can go out into the world and then come back and say 'Mark, I've met hundreds of people and I still love you most of all', I'll never have any doubts."

"If I do go I shall come back and say just that."

"God knows I'll be waiting for that day. But if you say it you must mean it."

He went to the window and stood looking out. "This island dominates my life. Through my father-in-law I hated it, every inch of it. Through you I'm growing to love it. Yet it will be a sad place when you have left. Every part of it will remind me of you. Write to me often, Ann. I know you'll not write what you don't feel and from your letters I'll know if you still love me."

I went to stand beside him. "If I do go, and remember I haven't agreed to yet, I'll write to you every day for you'll always be in my thoughts. And never doubt my love for you."

He smiled down at me but his eyes were sad. "This island is bewitched. It has a power over me. It offers me happiness but when I reach out to take it it snatches it back. I'm so afraid this new happiness is not to be."

I watched that strange haunted look spread over his face. "Mark," I said sharply in sudden fear. "What nonsense! And from a man who boasts he's old enough to know everything. The future can only have happiness for us. Unless you believe that I'll not leave you. I'll not go and leave you brooding here."

"You're right. I shall fill my days with my

writing and think only of the time when we'll be together again."

His mood was light again. "Let's have some music," he said, going across to the gramophone. "What shall it be? Mendelssohn's fairies? Grieg's trolls? What kind of creatures do I need to placate? They hide themselves from me – I'm just an intruder. But you must have seen them."

Now he was laughing at himself and I smiled.

"Peter will be home for the summer soon," he said, turning back from the gramophone. "Will you stay until he's home, Ann? I'll not feel our parting quite so much then."

"I'll wait until then," I agreed. "If I go."

"You must go, Ann. I'm sure it's the right thing to do."

"I must think it out for myself," I said obstinately, "I'll not be pushed into it."

"All right, my dear. But I warn you I'll be bringing all my pressures to bear on you if you don't come around to my way of thinking."

I knew that, in spite of everything, he wanted me to go and I knew in the back of my mind that I agreed with him. Yet some of his uneasiness had crept into me. The time seemed so long. So much could happen in three years. I shook myself out of this mood, realising that I was depressed at the thought of our parting. I would not share his silly superstition.

Chapter Fourteen

IT wasn't long before I decided that Mark was right and that I must go away. I couldn't tell my father that I was in love with him unless I could tell him the whole story and show him what kind of man Mark really was. This would mean Jenny telling him the truth about her baby. I couldn't be sure how he would take this and I couldn't risk him upsetting her so soon.

Besides, even if he knew everything about Mark, I felt that he would still not be pleased at the idea of my marrying him. He would object to his age, to the fact that he must be divorced first and most of all perhaps, even still, to Mark himself. For the two were like oil and water. I would rather keep the knowledge from him until it was possible for us to marry. Jenny might well be married herself by then too.

Equally well I knew that if I were not to tell I couldn't go on living at home and keeping it secret. It was an effort even to remember to refer to him as Mr Sutherby at home and in front of Mrs Willis and the others and to listen to them talking about him as if I had no interest in him.

And I knew that my father was watching me, waiting for me to tell him that I was leaving the island, as I had said I would.

"I've spoken to Mr Sutherby, Father," I told him. "About leaving I mean. He wants me to stay just until Peter comes home."

He looked at me sharply and for a moment I wondered what I'd said. "He won't be doing so much work while he has Peter with him," I added by way of explanation, trying to keep my manner natural.

"Well, I'll not deny that I'll be pleased to see you off the island," he said slowly. "But it'll not be the same here without you."

There was a plaintive note in his voice that moved me and for a moment I saw him as a lonely old man; Jenny married and absorbed perhaps in a young family, and myself – where would I be then? I felt a pang of remorse for wanting to leave him and a twinge of conscience for not telling

192

him why I was really going. But I had to stifle such thoughts. I had to lead my own life even if it did take me away from him.

When I told Mark that I had decided to go he was full of plans for me.

"You must go to Bob and Barbara. I'll write to them and fix it. They've got a huge old house and they'll be delighted to look after you and get you settled. They'll be surprised to hear from me. They'll love you for bringing me back to the fold as well as for yourself."

"And who are Bob and Barbara?" I asked, amused at the obvious satisfaction he felt at his idea.

"Bob's my best and oldest friend and his wife's one of the most charming people you could meet. I've treated them as badly as I did everyone else but they've always stuck by me. I haven't seen them for ages but they won't have changed."

"Well, it's very thoughtful of you, Mark, but I wasn't really planning on going as far as London to begin with. I assume they do live in London?"

"Where are you thinking of going then?"

"Well, I'd thought of starting off in Tollie."

It was Mark's turn to be amused and he

exploded into laughter.

"You're not serious? I thought you were out to see the world."

I looked at him soberly. "There's plenty of time. My father will miss me when I go and so will Jenny. I don't want to be so far away to begin with that I can't still see them. I'll move on when they get used to the idea."

"You love that rugged old father of yours, don't you, just as he does you. I remember the pride with which he spoke of you when we were discussing the idea of your coming to work for me. To tell you the truth I didn't care twopence then whether you were any of the things he said you were so long as you could type. It was only when you turned those grey eyes on me that I began to see that he was right. How could I help falling in love with you? You know Peter thinks the world of you too?"

"I'm glad if he does. Peter's a fine boy, Mark."

"I wonder if we'll get on together so well this time," he said anxiously.

"Of course you will. The more you see of each other the closer you'll become. He wants your love as much as you want his. You must know that as well as I do."

"I wish I felt as confident as you," he said rather gloomily. "Look, Ann, I know we agreed you would go when Peter came home, but will you stay on just a little longer? Just until we have time to get adjusted to each other again. You know what a moody person I can be even now. Things go more smoothly when you're around."

"Oh, Mark. You worry unnecessarily. There's nothing to worry about at all. Still, I don't mind, if that's what you want. I'm in no hurry to rush off and leave you as well you know. Besides, with a bit of effort we could get the book finished then. I'd like to see it finished before I go."

On the day when Peter was expected home I could see that Mark was nervous. He was going across in the boat to meet him and before he went I tried to ease his tension.

"Cheer up, Mark. This is a joyful occasion. For Heaven's sake remember to smile as soon as you see Peter. You're supposed to be welcoming him home remember."

He just gave me a look and went off without a word.

As soon as they came back I knew that everything was all right between them. Peter

195

came in to see me and say hallo and we greeted each other warmly. He was bubbling with youth and high spirits and Mark was quietly happy in the background watching us. I caught his eye and smiled and he smiled back, that warm smile that lit his whole face.

"It's great to be back here," Peter said enthusiastically, looking around him. "I've always liked it here. I've had some good times here but I've looked forward to it more this time than ever." He looked half-shyly at Mark as he said this and I saw the answering flash in Mark's eyes. I felt a lump come in my throat as I watched them.

"Well, let's go and attack some of that luggage of yours and get you settled in," Mark said, and they went off together.

With Peter's coming the old house seemed to light up. He was full of ideas, enthusiasms and plans. He was bursting with energy and whereas before the house had seemed so large and empty now it seemed filled. The two of them went sailing once or twice but, like me, Mark was keen to get the book finished and away before I left.

"I'll spend the rest of the summer with Peter then," he said, "and start on the new one when he goes back."

All that was left now was some tidying up and revising, and when the weather was good we took our work out of doors. A favourite spot of Mark's was a rocky promontory not far from the house. If the day was still and calm we spread a rug on the grass on the top but if there was any wind, especially the strong wind that blew down the loch at times, we moved from the top to the shelter of the rocks half-way down.

From either spot we could watch Peter as he swam or fished or pottered about in the small boat. He loved the water and was an expert swimmer. He would dive, too, from the rocks, for the water was deep all round the headland. Sometimes he would come up and lie in the sun with us, after swimming. And sometimes he'd be below us in the boat, shouting up to us from the water. The work was constantly interrupted but neither of us cared. If I'd still been just Mark's secretary my conscience might have troubled me at the little I did, but now it seemed like a gloriously happy holiday. We talked a lot about ourselves and the things we planned to do together.

One day when Peter was up on the promontory talking to us before going for a swim he went to the edge and looked over.

"Who dares me to dive off here?" he asked.

Mark got up and went to the edge and looked down.

"Not me," he said. "Too risky. I don't like the look of those rocks."

"And certainly not me," I said, without even going over to look.

"I'd be clear of the rocks from here," Peter said. "Bit high though, isn't it."

Mark turned away without saying any more and came back to sit down and I saw that his face had gone white. Peter hesitated on the edge and I knew that he was in two minds about doing it. In the end his youth won, he would not admit defeat. I watched him poise himself for the dive and I heard Mark draw a sharp breath. When I looked at him he'd closed his eyes.

Peter was gone and in a moment we were both at the cliff edge looking over. Peter was in the water well clear of the rocks. He had already surfaced and when he saw us he held his hands clasped above his head in a gesture of victory.

Mark turned away looking very shaken.

"Why didn't you stop him?" I said.

"Just because I'm a coward I don't have

to turn him into one. All the same I hope he doesn't try *that* again."

He let out his breath in a long sigh. "He's got more pluck than I have. Nothing would induce *me* to dive from there."

Later that day when I was back in the house typing up a few altered pages, Peter came in to talk to me.

"The book's almost finished now, isn't it," he said.

"Yes, there's very little left to be done."

He stood eyeing the manuscript. "What a lot of work there is in it. I hadn't thought much about his writing before. It means a lot to him, doesn't it? I mean he's terribly enthusiastic about it."

"Well, yes," I said, smiling. "It's really his main interest. And I think he's very pleased with *this* book."

"Oh, yes. He thinks it's a great success."

He watched me for a little while in silence, then he said, "He says you'll be leaving him when it's finished."

"Yes, that's right," I said, looking at his serious face.

"I wish you didn't have to go. So does my father, I can see he does. Do you have to go?"

"Yes, I'm afraid I do," I said gently,

touched by the look on his face. "I'll be sorry to go, Peter, and I'll miss you both. I've been very happy here. But I really only came for a short while."

He went and sat down in the chair, leaning forward with his elbows on his knees.

"My father will be lonely here," he said without looking up.

"Oh, but he has you," I said quickly.

"I mean when I go back. My mother will never come to live here. She hates the house and the island. But it isn't just that. They mean nothing to each other – my parents. I've known it for a long time."

I didn't know quite what to say to him. I went over and put a hand on his shoulder.

"I don't know your mother, Peter. But I do know that your father loves you very much. Never forget that."

"Yes. I know that now," he said. "And I think that my mother does too. I used to think that they didn't. I suppose it's just that I'm really an embarrassment to them – the way things are, I mean."

"Not any longer," I said. "Not now you understand the situation."

"There are some things I don't understand for all that."

"You will, in good time, I don't doubt.

Why don't you just take things as they come. Begin by enjoying your holiday with your father for instance."

He turned his boyish grin on me. "I'm doing that already."

When I was walking home from the boat with my father he too raised the subject of my leaving the island.

"Young Peter's been home a while," he said. "Isn't it time to be looking for another job?"

"Yes, I will now, Father."

"Well, if you're *really* looking," he said, giving me a hard look, "you needn't be looking far. There'll be the job going in the office over at the hospital with Wallace's niece getting married. You could have seen that for yourself. You've only to have a word with the doctor. He's over there most days. He'll speak for you."

"I'll go and see him after surgery," I said.

When I went up to bed that night a short time after Jenny I found her lying on her bed propped up on her elbow, still fully dressed. She watched me in silence for a minute or two as I put one or two things away, then she said quietly:

"Are you really going?"

I went and sat down on the edge of my

bed close to her and looked at her serious face.

"Will you mind very much?"

"I shall miss you if you go. But I wasn't thinking of that."

"What were you thinking of then?"

"Father doesn't believe you'll go, does he? He's waiting for you to think of another excuse to put him off."

"What on earth do you mean? Why shouldn't he believe me?"

"He thinks you're in love with Mr Sutherby. I can tell by the way he watches you and the things he says."

I felt the blood rush to my cheeks.

"You *are* in love with him too, aren't you?"

"Yes. I am."

"Oh, Ann. I guessed it too." She sat upright, staring at me with a woebegone face.

"Jenny, it's no tragedy. It's the most wonderful thing that could happen to me."

"How can you say that? It's not as if you can marry him."

"Not yet, it's true. But I will, before too long."

"You mean he'll be getting a divorce? Then he's in love with you too."

"Sh . . . Keep your voice down." I got up from the bed and walked around the room, wondering how much I should tell her.

I went back and sat beside her. "Jenny, now you know so much there are one or two things I should tell you. But you must keep it to yourself."

I told her as briefly as I could the part of Mark's story that now concerned me.

"So you see why I have to go away and why I don't want to tell father yet."

"I'm glad you told me. I hated to think of you going away unhappy. At least you have something to look forward to. It seems strange, though. You marrying Mr Sutherby. He always liked you, didn't he? Mrs Willis used to say so. Do you think Father will ever get to like him?"

"Perhaps he will, when he knows what he's really like. But it won't matter then. I shall marry Mark in any case. All the same it would be nice to have Father's blessing. Still, that day's a long way off yet."

I sat looking at her with affection, glad now that I'd been forced to share my secret with her. Yet I still couldn't bring myself to tell her what my father had suspected of Peter. Time will take care of that too, I thought.

Chapter Fifteen

THE manuscript was at last finished, all but the final checking and putting together, and since the weather continued fine we took the rug out to the headland and settled down to work there. The morning was still and calm but in the early afternoon a light breeze sprang up which soon freshened considerably, trailing long wisps of cloud across the sky.

Peter had been lying beside us sunbathing and reading and soon he sat up rubbing his arms. "It's getting chilly here now," he said. "I think I'll go for a swim. Anyone coming?"

"Not in that icy water," Mark said. "It needs to be warm to tempt me."

Peter just grinned at him and went off.

The checking was finished and I piled the typewritten sheets and some odd notes that Mark had been making back in the folder. "It won't take long to make those alterations," I said. "I'll get it ready to send away."

"Not this afternoon," Mark said, stretching back lazily on the rug. "Don't go indoors now. It'll probably be raining tomorrow."

I put the folder on the grass beside me and lay back on my elbows looking out over the loch. How perfect the last week or so had been. Soon it would be over and I'd be here no more. I was going to be very lonely without Mark. I turned to look at him. He was lying with his head on his clasped hands, looking up at the sky.

"With you and Peter here I have everything I want," he said.

"Are you telling me that you'd be quite happy to stay here now, even when there's no longer any need?" I said teasingly.

"Perhaps. If we could stop the clock at a chosen moment and say 'Let it be like this for ever'. But time won't stand still. Nor will human nature. Why must we always be so restless, even when we're happy. Sometimes we're not even aware of our happiness until it's passed. But I'm aware of it now, Ann. Very much aware of it. Perhaps it's because I know that soon it must end – for a time, at any rate. I certainly didn't expect to be so happy again."

He sat up and turned towards me. "Peter's growing up fast. He's full of ideas and ambitions for the future. He's got the youth, and soon he'll have the money, to go ahead with them. He'll need to live his own life and I wouldn't want it otherwise. We're very different from each other in lots of ways. I want the simple life – just my writing and you." He smiled across at me. "Do I make it sound very dull for you?"

"You make it sound so attractive I don't know how I'm going to wait."

Suddenly he reached over and pulled me to him, cradling my head against his shoulder.

"Oh, my dearest, how can I let you go?"

I stayed still in his embrace, the pleasure sharpened to pain by the knowledge that so soon I should be parted from him. How could I know that such a moment could have such terrible results.

As I sat there with his arms around me I heard the sound of stones crunched under someone's foot. Mark heard it too and he pushed me from him and looked over my shoulder. I turned my head and saw my father.

We both got to our feet as he moved towards us. He was carrying a spade across his shoulder and with a sudden, violent movement he flung it with all his force at our feet. I jumped back with a little cry of alarm and Mark put his hands on my shoulders and pulled me to him with a protective movement.

My father's eyes were blazing as they looked from one to the other of us. "I knew it," he said in a trembling voice. "Do you think I haven't guessed what's been going on there in the house? Now you even dare to bring it into the open."

Mark let me go and took a step towards my father. His face was hard and as white in its cold anger as my father's was red with passion.

"What are you doing here? How long have you been in the habit of spying on us?"

"Spying on you!" my father shouted. "Is it not a father's duty to protect his daughter from such a man as you are?"

"Stop it, Father," I said. "You've no idea what you're saying."

He turned on me. "I've listened to your lies long enough. You've never had any intention of leaving here. But you'll not be alone with him any more. I'll see to that."

He moved towards me as if to hustle me off there and then, but Mark stepped in front of him.

"If you were not so blinded by temper you'd see how contemptible your accusations are. Your daughter is incapable of the behaviour you suggest as you must know very well. Nor are *my* intentions dishonourable. In fact you might as well know now that I intend to marry Ann."

My father took a step backward with a quick intake of breath.

"That you'll never do, even if it were possible."

"That's not for you to say."

"No, it's for me to say," I said quickly. "I love Mark, Father, and I intend to marry him as soon as I can and you'll not stop me."

"And what about the wife he already has?" he demanded, turning on me again. "That's something you seem to be forgetting. Is it bigamy you're intending or are you letting him use you so that she will divorce him?" His eyes narrowed as they glared at me. "I've had one daughter behave like a trollop. As God is my witness I'll not let the other."

"I'll not listen to any more of this," Mark said angrily before I could answer. "There are many things you have the right to know about me. I'll admit that and I'm perfectly willing to tell you. But you'd better go away and get control of yourself first."

"And leave you alone with my daughter?" my father said furiously. "Oh, no, not any more."

He made a wild grab at me and Mark, losing control of himself, took him by the shoulders and shook him.

"By God, if you don't take yourself off from here until you can control your temper I'll not answer for the consequences."

My father pulled himself free with a furious jerk. "That's right. Swear by God. That's about all the use you have for Him. If you had a little religion in you, you wouldn't be the man you are."

His eyes went to the folder lying on the rug and his mouth twisted in scorn. "Books! A fine excuse for an idle life. Who would want to read anything you write? Your ideas would corrupt anyone, the way they've corrupted my daughter."

With a swift movement and before either of us could stop him he picked up the folder and hurled it towards the loch. It fell just short of the edge, scattering all its contents, and the wind started to whip them over the edge.

Mark stood like stone, his face white, watching the sheets blow away. I couldn't bear to see his work so destroyed and I started forward to save what I could. But Peter was there before me. He appeared as from nowhere, his bare feet making no sound on the grass. I had no idea how long he'd been there or how much he had heard.

Swiftly he picked up the folder and moved forward in a stooping position to collect the scattered papers. He was still wet from his swim. I saw the little rivulets of water running down his body as he bent there, silhouetted against the sky. I saw everything so clearly, as I still see it to this day. Suddenly his wet feet slipped on the grass or he trod on loose earth too near the edge, I couldn't be sure which. As he began to straighten up he lost his balance. He threw the bundle of papers from him in a frantic effort to save himself. Before any of us could help him he'd gone over the edge.

I heard myself scream his name. I heard Mark's agonized shout as he rushed to the edge. I saw him tear at his jacket and shoes. I saw him poised on the edge where Peter had dived. I watched him dive towards the water below. And all the time I couldn't move. I stared at the spot where Peter had been a few seconds before and I might have been made of stone.

I heard my father's voice near me, low, almost whispering. "I've killed him. God have mercy on me. I've killed him."

"No, Father. No," I said despairingly.

I remembered Mark's words about the rocks. Surely Peter had fallen clear. He was very close to the place where he'd dived.

My father's eyes looked at me and through me with a frightening expression in them. His greying hair blew in the wind. His lips moved ceaselessly, repeating over and over, "God have mercy on me. I've killed him."

I stared at him foolishly. Then at last I moved. Unceremoniously I pushed him down the hill. "Quick, Father. Go down to the water. I'll get help from the house."

I raced back to the house and found one of the men to take a boat across for the doctor. Two more of the men started off in the second boat for the headland. I burst in on Mrs Willis and gave her a distracted account of what had happened. Then I ran back again, my breath coming in painful gasps partly from the exertion but most of all from the terrible dread that filled me.

The news had spread quickly and several more of the men were already hurrying ahead of me. When I came to the beach before the headland I stopped dead. Mark was being helped from the water by the first of the men to arrive on the scene. Another man was wading ashore with Peter's limp

211

body in his arms.

I couldn't bear to look at Peter and I couldn't bear the look on Mark's face. I sank down on the beach where I was and covered my face in my hands.

There was a confusion of voices all round me and the tramp of feet on the stones. Presently a hand was laid on my shoulder and a man's voice said gently, "I'll take you back to the house, lass."

I looked up then to see one of my father's mates bending over me. And I saw the little procession moving slowly along the beach. One man holding Peter's still body followed by two others half-supporting, half-carrying Mark. The rest of the men straggled in a loose bunch behind. Far in the rear I saw my father with a man on either side of him supporting him by the arms. My eyes followed them along the beach.

"Come, lass," the man beside me said. "Let me take you back."

I shook my head slowly. "Let me stay. Please leave me alone."

He hesitated for a moment, then he said. "All right, lass. I'll leave ye for a bit. 'Tis a terrible shock it's been, I know. I'll send somebody out from the house."

I listened to his footsteps receding along

the beach. I stared up at the headland, seeing again the picture of Peter falling from the top. With a shudder of horror I turned my eyes away. When I looked at the water I saw Mark's face as he was helped out of it. Along the beach I saw the sad procession. There was nowhere I could look. I shut my eyes, covering my face with my hands again, willing myself not to think.

It was Meg who came looking for me. I heard her voice calling me a long way off as she scrambled over the rough ground. I thought she couldn't see me, crouched down as I was, but I had no will to stand up. I opened my mouth to call out to her but no sound came.

When she found me she fell on her knees beside me, flinging her arms around me. I stared at her tear-stained face in silence.

"He's dead," she blurted out, and she burst into heavy sobs, letting her head fall against my shoulder. I lifted my hand to smooth her hair and comfort her. I looked in wonder at the tears pouring down her cheeks. I felt my own cheeks. They were quite dry. I didn't want to cry. I didn't want to do anything.

"Oh, see me," she said at last, pushing herself away from me and fumbling for a

213

handkerchief to wipe her eyes. "It's me that should be taking care of you."

She scrambled to her feet and then helped me up. I let her lead me back to the house. I felt quite numb. Nothing was real to me. It was all a bad, dark dream.

I don't remember much else of what happened that day. All I can recall is being in a room, I think it must have been Mrs Willis's sitting room, with Mrs Willis and Dr Steven.

The next thing I remember is waking up as from a long, heavy sleep and finding myself in bed. I looked at the clock on the table beside me and it said almost ten o'clock. My first thought was that I'd over-slept. Why had nobody called me? Then I realised the clock wasn't mine and with a sudden rush of panic knew that I wasn't in my own room. My head felt heavy and I couldn't seem to think clearly. Then I remembered.

With a little cry I pushed back the bedclothes and started to get out of bed. Mrs Willis came forward from a chair where she'd been sitting and pushed me gently back into bed. "Not so fast," she said.

"It isn't true," I said desperately. "Tell me it isn't true."

214

She tried to soothe me while she covered me with the bedclothes again. I knew from her face that it was true.

"Aye, poor lad. There's many a sore heart'll be grieving for him today."

I buried my head in the pillow. If only I could go to sleep again, to sleep and forget this terrible feeling, to wake and find this nightmare had never happened. Then I remembered Mark's tortured face as he came up the beach. All these hours I'd left him alone! I must go to him, and at once.

Again I struggled to get out of bed, pushing Mrs Willis from me. And still she restrained me.

"I must see Mark," I said wildly. "You don't understand."

"I do understand," she said gently. "I know how things are between you. And certainly you must go to him as soon as you can, for if anyone can help him now it's you, my dear. But not yet, Ann, not yet."

Still I was impatient for her to let me go and then a thought struck me.

"Fiona? You mean Fiona's here?"

She shook her head. "We haven't been able to get in touch with Fiona. She's away at sea somewhere – on a cruise."

"Then why can't I go to him?"

"You'll be able to see him. All in good time. But remember you've had a terrible shock yourself. You need looking after too. Now be a sensible girl and you'll be away to see him in no time. First of all I'm going to fetch you a breakfast tray. Oh, you can manage a nice hot drink at any rate," she said as I started to refuse it. "You'll feel better for getting up then."

As soon as she'd left me I got out of bed and I was surprised to find how shaky my legs were and how dazed I still felt. I caught sight of my reflection in the mirror on the dressing table and for a moment I scarcely recognized myself. My face was very pale and there were great dark circles under my eyes as heavy as if they had been painted there. My hair was loose about my shoulders and the nightgown I was wearing, one of Mrs Willis's I guessed, hung from my shoulders in loose folds.

I sank back on the bed in dismay and waited for Mrs Willis to return. By the time I'd finished the drink she brought me and washed and dressed and combed back my hair I felt much better and some of the anxiety went out of Mrs Willis's face as she looked at me.

"You're a brave girl, Ann, and a sensible

one. You'll be all right. I wish I could say the same for Mr Sutherby and your father. They've taken it very badly, you'll find that out for yourself when you go in to see Mr Sutherby."

"I'll go and see him now," I said.

"The doctor said I was to keep you here quiet until he saw you again. He'll be across after surgery. He'll not be long."

"I'll not wait for the doctor," I said, shaking my head.

"Well, I can see for myself it's not going to help you, keeping you fretting here. You go along. He's in the study. I'll come and tell you when the doctor comes."

I went into the study through my own little room and found Mark sitting at his desk, staring in front of him. He was aware of my presence as I hesitated for a moment in the doorway and his eyes turned towards me. He looked old and tired and terribly sad. His eyes followed me as I crossed the floor towards him but his expression didn't alter and he didn't speak. I stood looking at him. What could I say? What could I do to comfort him? There are times when we seem utterly alone, no matter how close and how anxious to help and comfort are those around us. I knew that for Mark this was such a time. I went round behind him and put my arms round him, resting my head against his. Perhaps he found some comfort in my presence for after a while he took both my hands in his and held them tight and we stayed close together without speaking.

He had said something once about history repeating itself. How terribly it had repeated itself for *him*. Once before he had come to the island with the hope of finding love and happiness. Fiona's father had destroyed that hope then. Now he'd come back and found a new happiness and my father had taken it from him.

Much as I had laughed at his superstitious nonsense it was true that the island brought him nothing but unhappiness.

Chapter Sixteen

MRS WILLIS took me to her sitting room when Dr Steven arrived.

"You're doing fine," he said, looking at me critically. "Though you could look a deal better yet."

He sat me down beside him while he sipped the coffee Mrs Willis brought him. "This is indeed a sorry business," he said. "And if all I've been hearing is true, it's no wonder you took it so hard."

He sat looking at me for a moment or two. "Your father's taken it hard too, as well as Mr Sutherby. It's not a doctor that will cure either of those two."

I sat in silence, thinking of Mark. I could not bring myself to feel sorry for my father no matter how he felt now.

When Dr Steven stood up to go he put an arm around my shoulders and gave me a fatherly squeeze. "Take care of yourself, Ann. There's a time of strain ahead of you still. Come and see me if I can be of any help. And don't worry about your father. Jenny's at home with him."

After he'd gone Mrs Willis told me that she had a pile of the manuscript papers that someone had collected from the headland after the accident.

"I'll put them in the study some time when Mark is not there," I told her. "I don't suppose he'll want to be reminded of those for a while."

"There's one other thing too," she said. "The arrangements for the funeral have to be made. By the time Fiona gets the news of Peter's death it'll be too late for her to do anything about it. She'll not even be able to get here in time for the funeral. So I'm afraid we'll just have to go ahead without her. I don't like to bother Mr Sutherby with him as he is but we'll need to know if he'll agree to the arrangements before we can start making them. Will you speak to him or shall I?"

I told her that I would do so.

"The family have always been buried here on the island after a service over in the church, as you know of course. But Mr Sutherby has never set foot inside the church nor indeed taken any interest in it as the head of the family has done in the past. The minister did come across to see him when he first came to the island but I'm afraid he failed to persuade him. I don't believe they've ever met since."

I could see that she was anxious and I thought that she had reason to be. Apart from the service in the church, would Mark agree to Peter being buried here, I wondered.

Mark was still shut up in the study where he'd been all day. He'd moved from the desk to one of the chairs that faced the doorway so that as I opened the door I found him looking at me. His face had a terrible haunted look and I knew that all he did was sit there brooding.

"Mark," I said, going over to him, "I'm sorry to have to bother you about this now, but the arrangements for the funeral have to be made. Mrs Willis wants to know if it's all right to have the service over in the church and have Peter buried here on the island."

He looked at me for a long time before answering and I began to wonder if he had understood or even heard my question.

"Why not?" he said at last, and his voice was hard and bitter. "His burial must be all that Duncan Reddie would have given him. Let him lie in the burial ground beside his grandfather. He took him from me while he lived. Now he's taken him in death. He always knew he could better me. What a fool I was ever to think otherwise."

His words struck a chill in me.

"That's not true, Mark. Peter loved you and you know it. No matter what his grandfather did he couldn't stop that happening. Bury him here on the island, yes. But because he belongs here. Because he loved the island. It was his home, the home he shared with you."

I could see that my words meant nothing to him. He sat staring in front of him as if he were looking at something far away and he went on talking as if to an unseen audience.

"We have no control over our lives, much as we might think otherwise. Our path is set from the start and there's no turning aside. For a while I deluded myself into thinking that I could change my direction. Now I know how wrong I was. This was the inevitable end. Duncan Reddie brought me back here. He was the instrument to separate me from my son, one way or another. He was to destroy me. How well he succeeded."

I looked at his face, bitter and hopeless. I knew how much he'd longed to have Peter with him all the while he was growing up. I knew how happy he had been to know that he was close to him at last. I'd expected him to be shattered with grief now at his death. But I had not been prepared for this.

"Mark, how can you talk like that? Duncan Reddie had nothing to do with Peter's death. Nor can he destroy you. No one can. Only you can destroy yourself if you indulge these foolish fancies. But I won't let you, Mark. I love you and I won't let you."

"It's no use, Ann," he said, and his voice was as dead and hopeless as his face. "Don't you see that even our love is part of the inevitable pattern. It was my love for you that led to Peter's death. I killed him, just as surely as if I'd pushed him over on to the rocks."

"Oh no, Mark. No. You can't believe that."

He stood up and moved away from me. "I love you, Ann. I wanted to be free to marry you. But not at that price – not through Peter's death."

"Oh, Mark, do you think I don't know that? Do you think I want it that way either?"

He looked at me gloomily. "It would have been better if you'd never met me. I can only bring you unhappiness, as I have to everyone else I ever cared for."

"That's nonsense too, Mark. You've already brought me more happiness than I ever dreamed of."

He turned away from me without answering and I knew that nothing I could say or do then would ease his distress. He was still too close to yesterday's tragedy. It would take time before he saw everything in true perspective again.

I could see that he didn't really want my company now, that he wanted to be left alone, and feeling utterly miserable myself I went back to Mrs Willis.

She looked at me anxiously as I came in and sat down wearily. "You look all in," she said, her face full of kind concern. "You'll need to take things easy for a bit."

I told her that Mark agreed to the arrangements for the funeral.

"Look, Ann," she said. "Why not stay here for a day or two, at least until the funeral's over, and let me look after you? Your father will be all right with Jenny, I'm sure. I feel you have enough strain on you already. I'll send Meg across to explain things at home and bring over anything you might need."

I was grateful for her kindness and for her suggestion. As Mark recovered from the first shock, he might well need me and in any case, in spite of knowing that my father, too, was far from well, I had no wish to see him. I blamed him entirely for what had happened.

But Mark showed no signs of needing me, or indeed of wanting me near him. All he wanted was to be left alone and I could well imagine the thoughts that were turning over and over in his mind as he stayed shut in on himself. As time went by and he didn't change I was in almost as deep a despair as he was himself.

Although Mark had said in his bitterness that Peter should have the funeral that his grandfather would have given him, everything was done as simply and quietly as possible. There were no guests at the House and no friends or neighbours, for Mark had entered into no social life whatever since living there.

Two boats crossed from the island for the service in the church. The first one took the coffin and its bearers, with Mark sitting alone in the prow. I went in the following boat with Mrs Willis and Meg and one or two others.

Meg was crying audibly as we stood on the jetty watching the coffin being lifted into the boat and I saw tears in Mrs Willis's eyes too. But still I shed no tears myself. It was as if everything in me had been frozen up. Mark had spoken to no one, appearing only when it was time to leave. I could only guess at his feelings as he sat there in the boat, still and alone, cut off from any sympathy or comfort by his own choosing.

In my grief for Peter and my despair over Mark, I had forgotten what an event a funeral from the House was considered to be. Although I had not been to Duncan Reddie's, since I had been nursing my mother at the time, I knew it had been talked about for days in the village.

Now as the boats drew towards the shore I was dismayed by the number of people I saw gathered round the jetty. I had been shut away in the quietness of the House for the last few days and now I found it an ordeal to face so many curious eyes.

The church was full for the service and from the many people who spoke to me I realised how shocked and moved the village had been at the tragedy of Peter's death. Mark walked through them all with unseeing eyes and, looking at his face, they kept their distance.

As we left the church I saw Jenny waiting to speak to me. She looked pale and very distressed.

"I wanted to come and see you," she said. "Tom would have taken me across, but I don't like to leave Father for long. I've left Tom with him now."

"Tom?" I said in surprise.

She shrugged almost impatiently. "Father

226

knows everything now. But it doesn't make any difference. Nothing matters to him now. Oh, Ann. I know how you must feel. But come and see him. Come home when you can."

I was touched by the distress in her face and the fear in her voice. There was no time to stay and talk to her. The others were already ahead of me, going back to the jetty. "I'll come," I promised.

The coffin was lifted once more into the boat and we started on the journey across the loch, watched by the silent people on the jetty. The minister went back with us in the second boat and Mark returned as he had come, sitting alone in the first.

We stood in a small group around the newly dug grave while the minister read the burial service. Above his quiet voice I could hear the water lapping the rocks below and the wind rustling the leaves of the tall trees. I remembered when I'd stood there before, looking at Duncan Reddie's grave, when Mark and I had met for the first time. It seemed so long ago now, so much had happened in between. I looked across at Mark where he stood apart from the rest of us, but his eyes never left Peter's coffin. As soon as the service was over he turned and walked away.

We went back to Mrs Willis's sitting room and Meg brought in some tea. The minister stayed only a short time and while Mrs Willis was showing him out I went along to the study to see if Mark was there. The door from my little room was locked and so was the door into the hall. I hesitated for a moment with my hand on the doorknob, but I didn't call to him nor ask him to open the door. He had deliberately shut himself away from me and I was more hurt than I had thought possible. Mrs Willis came back into the hall as I stood there and guessing what had happened, slipped an arm around me and led me back to her room.

"Don't lose heart, my dear. This is a black day for him."

She drew me down into a chair. "Why don't you go home tonight, Ann. I doubt if Mr Sutherby will want anything from anyone and I'll keep an eye on him."

I didn't want to go home but I didn't want to stay in the House either. In fact there was nothing I did want to do. I think that I too had reached the depths of my despair and unhappiness.

Mrs Willis was watching me. "I saw you

talking to Jenny, Ann, so I guess you know all about your father. He blames himself for Peter's death. It's a terrible weight of guilt for a man like him to have on his mind. Dr Steven is afraid it will affect his reason. I didn't like to tell you before, you had so much on your own mind. It might help if you go home and see him. Try and persuade him from his way of thinking. It was a terrible thing to happen. But it was an accident, and he was really no more to blame than anyone else. God knows he wouldn't have wanted it to happen."

I pushed my hand wearily through my hair. "Yes, I will go home," I said. "Jenny is very upset, I could see."

She pulled a footstool over to my feet. "Just you sit back and rest here quietly for a while. I'll get the house boat to take you across, and Meg can go with you."

I sat there thinking over what she had said. My father blamed himself for Peter's death. I too had blamed him. Yet Mark had said that he had caused it. If my father had not lost his temper it would not have happened. If Mark and I had not given way to our feelings it would not have happened either. Were we not all to blame? I realised now that it was not just one isolated incident

229

that had led to it. My father had always disliked and mistrusted Mark. Yet if he'd known all the truth, would he have felt such a need to protect me from him? I had kept so much from him. It had seemed right at the time. Now I was not so sure. I was no longer sure about anything.

Meg came for me after a while and we went down to the boat together. Her mood was as sombre as mine and our journey across the loch was a silent one, for which I was thankful. I was glad of her company when we came ashore, for she took my arm and marched me straight past anyone we met, giving them no time to stop and speak. At the door of our house she let go of my arm, giving it a squeeze as I thanked her for coming.

"I hope your father will be all right. I know Jenny will be thankful to see you."

I turned towards the door. It seemed so long a time since I was last there. I might have been a stranger, for there was no feeling of warmth in me to be coming home.

Chapter Seventeen

JENNY must have heard me open the door, for as I stepped inside she poked her head round the kitchen door. Then she came hurrying to meet me, still wiping her hands on the kitchen towel.

"I thought it couldn't be Tom. Oh, I'm so glad you've come. You don't know how relieved I am."

She pushed the tumbled hair back from her forehead with the towel and looked at me with sympathy. "You must be feeling terrible."

I started to take off my jacket and she took it from me and hung it on one of the pegs as if she thought I was incapable of doing it myself.

"Where's Father? Is he in bed?"

"Not him. He's never been one to stay in his bed, has he? I don't know why he feels he must get up though. There's nothing he wants to do. He just sits there all the time."

She pointed to the living room and I turned towards the door, but she stopped me with a hand on my arm.

"Come into the kitchen first and let me get you some tea. You look as if you can do with something."

I shook my head. "I had some tea at the House."

She still kept her hand on my arm, holding me back.

"You'll get a shock when you see him. He's so strange. He doesn't speak. In fact he takes no notice of anything that goes on. Oh, Ann, he frightens me. Sometimes I think he's going out of his mind."

"I'll go in and see him," I said, turning again towards the living room.

She didn't follow me. "I'm just starting the supper," she said. "Not that he eats anything. But you'll be needing something, so I'll just go back and finish it."

My father sat in a chair beside the empty fireplace, his hands lying idle in his lap, his eyes staring into space. He was grey-faced and haggard. I stood in the doorway looking at him, still with that frozen feeling inside me, so that I couldn't feel the concern for him that Jenny showed.

I closed the door behind me and walked slowly into the room. At first he made no move, but as I stood in front of him he moved his eyes so that they rested on my face. At first there was a frightening emptiness in them. No hostility now, no anger, and no warmth either. I thought that he didn't recognize me. Then, as he continued to look at me, I saw his face change. A look of pain crossed it and his eyes changed too, taking on that haunted look that I'd seen in Mark's. He brushed his hand across his face as if to drive away something that troubled him. There was something pathetic about the gesture. My father, once so sure of himself, so strong-minded and forceful, seemed now no more than a child.

I sat down in the chair across from him and we sat there in silence, looking at each other.

"So you've come home," he said at last in a flat voice. "He wants no more of you after what I've done."

"No, Father, that's not right. Mark's love for me is real. Not the kind that you'd imagined. It wouldn't stop because of anything *you'd* done."

"Then why have you left him?"

"I haven't left him. I'm going back."

"Why did you come? To remind me in case I'd forgotten? To sit there and haunt me?"

His eyes now had a wild light in them and I saw that he was trembling as he leaned towards me.

"No, Father. That's not why I came."

He leaned back in his chair as if he was exhausted, yet his eyes still watched me.

"*He* sent you across then. What has he sent you to tell me?"

"He didn't send me across and he hasn't anything to tell you. He doesn't blame *you* for Peter's death. He blames himself."

He sat up again in his chair and his eyes opened wide in disbelief.

"Then his reason's gone. It was me who killed the lad. You know that. I murdered him."

"Don't say that, Father," I said sharply. "You had no intention of harming Peter. It was an accident, and you know it."

"Aye. But the result's the same. His death's on my mind. It's something I can't forget."

His eyes reflected the torture of his thoughts, thoughts which could drive him to madness, as Jenny feared.

"You're no more to blame than anyone else," I said, leaning towards him. "We're equally to blame, all three of us. And there's not one of us that wouldn't have given anything to prevent it happening."

I got up from my chair, tortured now by my own regrets. "Oh, why did we have to get to such a state? Why didn't I tell you everything? That I really loved him and he loved me. If I'd told you, Father, what kind of man Mark really is you wouldn't have felt towards him as you did."

My father looked at me with hurt and bewilderment in his eyes. "Aye, why didn't you tell me? There's a lot you kept from me. Young Jenny too. You knew it was Tom Mellor's baby, didn't you? Did you think her father had no right to the truth?"

"I was thinking of Jenny's happiness, Father. Without Tom she'd have been completely miserable. I didn't think you'd see that. I wasn't even sure that you'd care."

He made no answer to that.

"I've only done what I thought was best for you both," he said, after a while. "What went wrong, lass? When your mother was alive we were all close to each other. Things have not been the same since she died."

I was unexpectedly moved by his words and by the sadness in his voice. I put my arm around his shoulder. He seldom mentioned my mother and never seemed to dwell on the past. But now I knew that Jenny and I had never filled the gap her death had left in his life. He still needed her.

And suddenly I needed her too. I wanted

235

the days when I could run to her for comfort in my troubles, for now they were too much for me to bear alone. With startling suddenness the tears came and great sobs shook my body. I fell at my father's feet, burying my head in his lap.

I felt Jenny's hands on my shoulders trying to raise me up and I heard my father's voice stop her.

"Leave her be, lass. Let her cry it out."

I sobbed until I was exhausted and there were no more tears to come. At last I was quiet and too tired to move.

Jenny spoke to my father in a low voice and I didn't hear what she said.

"She'd be best off in her bed now," he answered. "She's worn herself out."

I was in fact thankful to get to bed. She helped me in and brought me a hot drink, for I said I was too tired to be bothered with anything else. She sat on the bed while I sipped it.

"It's done Father good – you coming home. I can hardly believe the difference in him."

She took my empty cup and settled the bedclothes around me. "I'll leave you to sleep. It's what you need. I might get Father to eat some supper tonight."

I think I was asleep almost before she had left the room. I slept well and when I woke the next morning I felt better for it. Jenny was already up and I lay for a while thinking, trying to look calmly and clearly at the future.

I was just about to get up when Jenny looked in. "Oh, you're awake," she said. "I've got a tray ready for you. Wait a minute, I'll bring it up."

She disappeared before I could argue and I settled back in bed again. It wasn't until I smelled the bacon that she brought in that I realised how hungry I was.

She sat at the bedside talking to me while I ate.

"You're looking better this morning. Father's better too. He's had some breakfast. He's asked me several times if you're awake yet."

"Yes. I hadn't realised it was so late. What about your job? I suppose Miss Lang can manage for a while."

"Oh, yes. She told me to stay away as long as I needed to. As a matter of fact, though, I won't be going back there any more. I'll be needing to go and tell her."

I looked at her in surprise.

"Tom's parents know about me and Tom.

He's told them he wants to marry me. I'm going to work in the shop with Tom and his father. His mother can take things more easy then."

I saw the quiet happiness in her face and I was happy for her sake.

"I'm glad about that. Father will be too, I'm sure. He knows how you feel about Tom. He knows about the baby too now, doesn't he? He seems to accept it quite calmly. That at least is something to be thankful for."

"That's the strange part about it," she said with a small frown of puzzlement. "I wonder if he really does know?"

"What do you mean? I thought it was you who told him."

"It was, but I wonder if he remembers. You see, when he first came home, after the accident, he talked a lot – almost as if he was delirious. He kept on about you being mixed up with a married man. He kept saying it couldn't be right, no matter what you said. I thought it might ease his mind if I told him what you told me, since there was no point in keeping it from him any longer. That was when he went all quiet and wouldn't talk at all. Tom knew how worried I was about him and he used to go and sit with him and try to get him to talk. One day after Tom had gone he suddenly said, 'It was Tom's baby, wasn't it?' I told him it was and he didn't say any more. He's never mentioned it since, even when Tom's been here."

"Well, he does remember. He told me he knew when we were talking yesterday. But it's a small matter to him now, I expect, besides Peter's death."

"I'm glad he knows, it's a great relief. I was always afraid he'd ask me.

"What about Mr Sutherby?" she asked presently. "He looked terrible yesterday. I suppose he'll never forgive Father. It's a terrible thing between them."

"He doesn't blame Father. He blames himself."

I saw the disbelief in her face, just as I'd seen it in my father's. "We were all to blame, Father no more than us. It was a terrible end to our quarrels and our misunderstandings. Jenny, there's something I haven't told you yet. Father thought the baby was Peter's, and I let him go on thinking it."

She drew away from me in shock. "I suppose it was because he'd seen you dancing with Peter that day in the garden."

"But why did you let him think it?"

"I could only convince him that it wasn't

239

by telling him it was Tom's. I always meant that we should tell him the truth as soon as . . ."

"I can see why you did it," she said quickly before I could finish, "you did it for me, because I was too much of a coward to face the consequences. Oh, Ann, if he'd known the truth . . ."

She broke off, staring at me with a face that was full of distress and I knew what she was thinking.

"It wouldn't have made any difference," I said, trying to soothe her. "Our quarrel was older and deeper than that. Father has never liked nor understood Mark and I did nothing to help him to understand."

"All the same," she said, "it's frightening to think how the things we do can affect so many other people. I'd never thought about it before."

"We've all been learning that lesson. We could wreck all our lives now with regrets and recriminations. But what good would that do to anybody? Certainly none to Peter. None of us will forget what has happened. But even so, we've got to live for the future now, every one of us."

"What will you do now?" she asked me, after a while.

240

I thought of Mark, shut away from me in the House. "I don't know. We haven't had much chance to talk about the future yet."

"What about Father? They're all sorry for him, aren't they? Do you think he'll ever go back to the island?"

"I don't know. I've been wondering about that too. He'll need to do something, and the sooner the better."

She sighed. "Everything seems such a mess. I'm glad you're home."

"I must get up," I said, pushing back the bedclothes. "Thanks for the breakfast. It was just what I needed."

"What are you going to do today?" she asked, as she picked up the tray and went to the door.

"Not much by the look of it. It's pretty late already."

"You're not going across to the island?"

"No. I don't think there's anything I can do over there today and I want to have a talk with Father."

"Well, if you're going to be home with Father, I'll go down and do some shopping and call in to see Miss Lang too."

"Go and see Tom's family, too," I called after her. "They'll be pleased to see you and you've nothing to hurry back for."

"Aye. Maybe I will," she called back.

When I went downstairs I found my father in the living room leaning against the mantelpiece. He turned round as soon as I opened the door and I suspected that he'd been wandering restlessly around the room, waiting for me to come down.

"You slept well," he said. "Jenny looked in on you several times."

"Yes, I did," I said, "and I feel much better for it."

I sat down in the chair beside the fireplace and after standing looking at me for a moment my father sat down in the other one, leaning forward on his elbows. He looked tired and still very haggard, but at least he had some life in his face now and in his eyes.

"You're not going across to the House?"

"Not today. The day's nearly half over in any case."

"What will *he* do now?"

I knew he was thinking of Mark. "I'm not sure yet. But I don't think he'll be staying on the island for long."

He got up and began to move restlessly around. "Jenny was spinning me some long story one day here. She said she got it from you. It seemed to me there wasn't much truth in it."

"It was all true, Father. Mark told me himself."

"And you believe him?"

"Yes, I do."

My father grunted. "So, according to him, he and Fiona have been living apart for years."

He came and stood in front of me. "Now, I suppose, he can have his divorce."

I nodded, thinking of Mark's words about not wanting his freedom in exchange for Peter's life, and I wondered how long it would be before he could bring himself to think about the question of divorce.

My father stood considering me for a long while in silence. "How do you know old Duncan Reddie wasn't right?" he asked at last. "Perhaps he did want to marry Fiona for her position and her money."

"Well, he can hardly be wanting to marry me for mine," I said, refusing to be drawn into that discussion.

My father looked at me from under his shaggy eyebrows for a moment or two. "He has no religion and no respect for doing what's right, that's what I hold against him. He hasn't much of a conscience either."

"He has a religion, of sorts, Father,

though you might not recognize it as such. And he certainly has a conscience."

"If he had a conscience he'd not have married Fiona in the first place, knowing well he couldn't afford to keep her in the way she had a right to expect."

"It was Fiona's choice, as well as his. She knew his position, it wasn't as if he hid it from her. She didn't have to marry him."

My father was looking at me closely. "Didn't she? Why should she go rushing off to marry him like that? Young Peter was born pretty soon after they were married, wasn't he?"

I stared at my father. "Is that what you believed?"

"Everyone here believed it. It was a pretty bad shock for her father, I can tell you, coming so soon after his wife's death too."

"Well, I don't believe it. And if her father put that story around, or even allowed it to be rumoured, he was even worse than I thought he was. They'd never have married in such a hurry, perhaps not even at all, if he hadn't driven Fiona away by trying to force her to marry somebody she didn't want to."

"Duncan Reddie was a fine man, and

don't you be saying otherwise. He had a duty to his daughter and to his family."

"It's no one's duty to impose their will on somebody else regardless of their wishes. Not even a father's."

My father looked at me in silence for a moment or two. "That's what you've been thinking about me, I suppose?"

"Well, I think I'm old enough now to be able to think things out for myself," I said slowly. "And after all, we don't all see things or even people with the same eyes. But I'm beginning to see now why you've always distrusted Mark. But he's not at all the kind of person you thought he was."

He didn't say any more for a long time and presently he came and sat down again.

"He'll go back to England now, most likely," he said, looking across at me.

"Yes, I expect he'll go to London."

"What will you do?"

"I'll go to London too. I'll get myself a job down there for a while – until we're able to get married."

"Are you sure, lass, that you're doing the right thing?" he asked me, and I could see the doubt and anxiety in his face.

"Yes, Father, I'm quite sure," I said firmly.

"Well, I never did take to him and I'm not going to pretend now," he said. "He's still not the man I would have liked to see you marry. You'd be better with someone your own age, someone who's not been married before. Someone more like yourself. In fact, almost anybody else. But I suppose I'm wasting my time telling you so."

Again he got up from his chair and took a few turns around the room. Then he came back and stood looking down at me. "I still think you'll be making a mistake to marry him. But I'm interfering no more. If you think you'll be happy with him then I'll not be the one to stand in the way. God knows, I've harmed the man enough already. But be sure, be very sure first."

"I'll have plenty of time for that, Father, in any case, for it'll be some time before he can think about marrying."

"London's a long way off," he said with a sad note in his voice. "When you go there you'll be lost to me. I'll not see you again."

"Oh yes you will," I said emphatically. "Though you must give me time to save up the fare. I'll want to come back and see you, and I will."

He sighed. "Why did you have to choose somebody who takes you so far away? Was there no likely lad in the village for you?"

"No, Father. There wasn't. And I would have gone anyway, for you know I've always wanted to.

"What will you do, Father?" I asked him. "Will you go back to the island? Your job means a lot to you, doesn't it?"

"I don't know yet," he said slowly. "There may be changes over there now. We shall have to wait and see. But if not that job, there'll be some other. I shall work, I hope, until the day I die. And I shall keep this house. This is my home. Jenny can marry her Tom when she wishes. I'll be dependent on no one."

I could not resist a smile, for now he looked his old self. His chin was stuck out aggressively and his eyes looked at me with defiance. I stood up beside him and, putting my arms around his neck, pulled his face down to mine.

"You'll always have Jenny near you, even when she's married," I said. "And I'll come home for the wedding."

"Aye, you do that, lass," he said, holding me to him for a moment. "You'll be needing some fresh air in your lungs by then anyway."

Chapter Eighteen

WHEN I went back to the island I was in a much more hopeful mood than when I had left it. By going home I had found both comfort and a new strength, although I had not thought to find either.

When I arrived at the House, Mr Martin, the estate manager, was in with Mrs Willis, but she left him to come to speak to me. "I'm glad to see you looking better. How is your father now?"

I told her that he was almost his old self again and asked about Mark.

She hesitated a moment before answering. "He's packing up to leave," she said, watching me to see how I would take the news. "In fact I'm relieved to see you back, for I think he'll be going before the day's out."

This was, in fact, no more than I had expected.

I found him in the study removing his books from the shelves. He didn't hear me coming, for as I approached the doorway between our rooms, a row of books fell sideways with a clatter, where he'd removed their neighbours. I stood in the doorway for a moment watching him, wondering how he would be.

As he turned from the bookshelves he caught sight of me and stopped dead and for a moment the old look of warmth at seeing me was on his face. Looking at him then I knew that no matter what he said or did, he still loved me. Yet even as I started across the floor to him, I watched his face change. His eyes, which in that first moment of seeing me had been wide and welcoming, now peered at me through the shutters of his sandy lashes. The reserve in his face made me stop short of him.

"I thought you'd gone," he said accusingly.

"It looks as if *you* soon will be," I said, looking at the half-empty bookshelves.

"Yes. I want to get off this cursed island before I lose my reason altogether."

He dumped the pile of books he was holding beside a stack on the floor, then straightened up again.

"In any case, I'm just trespassing now. Our friend Duncan made that quite clear. He thought of everything, as you can imagine. Perhaps he thought I might be tempted to take a holiday here, or even hope to go on living here rent free."

"What are you talking about?" I said.

"Martin is now in charge of everything until the new Lord of the Island arrives. I am no longer required. Duncan, at this stage, washes his hands of me."

"Well, I shouldn't think that's going to upset you. Who's coming here?"

"The same cousin, or second cousin, whatever he was, whom Fiona refused to marry. And so the proud name of Reddie will still be here, in spite of my little interference in Duncan's schemes. Can't you just hear him, Ann, out there, settling in his grave with a sigh of satisfaction? He's done what he wanted. He can afford to let me off the hook now. The miserable little fish has taken its last gasp."

"Oh, for heaven's sake, Mark," I said, looking at his moody face. "Duncan Reddie's dead, finished with you, like you said. Why can't you be finished with him? That devil's ridden you long enough. Leave it here on the island, buried along with Duncan himself. Then you might find something worth living for again."

He turned away from me, saying nothing.

"I know how much you loved Peter, how you feel about losing him," I went on. "But you are deliberately building this into something other than grief, just as you are deliberately shutting the door against any future happiness you might have. Duncan Reddie had an obsession that dominated his life, as you once pointed out to me. But you have an obsession too, Mark. Are you going to let that wreck the rest of your life, now that he no longer can? And mine too, for that matter. I love you, Mark, and we could still find happiness together if you would let us."

Still he made no answer and he still kept his back turned to me.

"In any case," I ended by saying, "do you think Peter would want it this way either? It was your real self he loved and respected, Mark, not the man you have become."

He turned on me then with a flash in his eyes that made me wonder if I'd gone too far. He stood glaring at me for a minute or two, then without a word he turned back to the books.

In silence we stacked the books and records and other knick-knacks on the floor to be packed up and sent after him. Then he turned to the desk. I watched him as he sifted through the papers, setting them in order for Mr Martin to take over. Now he was business-like, his brooding and his nervous excitement gone. The sooner he has a purpose in life again, I thought, the better.

There were some letters to be answered too and we dealt with them together as we had been used to. When he had finished with the estate business, he turned to the other side of the desk where he kept all his personal papers and notes in connection with his writing and I took the letters into my room to be typed later on.

When I came back he was standing staring into the top drawer which he had pulled open and I could see at once that something had upset him again. Too late I remembered the manuscript sheets I'd put there one day when he was out of the study. Until now I'd completely forgotten them, so many other things had been on my mind.

With a fierce gesture, he yanked the drawer right out and tipped its contents into the wastepaper basket. Then he pulled open the next drawer, intending, it seemed, to do the same. I moved around the desk before he could do so and leaned against the drawer, preventing him.

"I'll clear your desk and sort your papers for you," I said quietly. "I'll get them packed up to be sent on with your other things."

For a moment he stood there, reaching down to the drawer still, his face close to mine. Then with a shrug he turned away.

"There's no need for that," he said. "Just throw the lot away."

I picked out the papers and notes from the wastepaper basket and put them back again into the drawer. He watched me with an expressionless face. "You're wasting your time."

"I can understand you feeling that way now," I said. "But you won't always. You've not finished writing, Mark, any more than you've finished living."

He didn't answer and presently he turned away and walked out of the room. I went and typed out the letters and laid them on his desk, and he still hadn't returned. Since it was almost lunchtime, I went along to find Mrs Willis.

"What will happen here now?" I asked her. "Will things still go on as usual, do you think?"

"For the time being, nothing will change, except that Mr Martin will now be in charge of the estate. When the new master comes I don't know what will happen. We'll just have to wait and see. It may be some time before he comes though, for I understand he's living abroad somewhere at the moment."

"He's a cousin or a relative of some kind of Duncan Reddie, isn't he? Is he married?"

"Oh yes. I think he married some years ago. I don't know whether he has any family. There may be quite a few changes when he comes. In the house, too, I mean. For myself I don't mind. I'm getting a bit old now to keep going as I do and I'm not sure that I'll want to stay on under the new owners even if the job is offered to me. But I hope the men at any rate will keep their jobs, for there'd be no alternative for most of them, short of leaving the village. Their lives are bound up here."

"Like Father," I said.

"I was going to ask you about your father. Mr Martin was talking about him this morning. He thinks very highly of him, you know. His job's still here for him, of course. Do you think he'll come back?"

"I don't know. I've an idea he will though. He's as much pride in this place as if he owns it."

"Most of them feel like that. Almost like a family. It's always been a good place to work. Old Mr Duncan may have been a bit of a dictator, but he was always respected and admired. He was a man who knew his own mind and I think the men thought all the more of him for that. You never heard any complaints from them in his day."

She stopped, looking slightly confused, and I smiled. "You mean there have been since. Well, it's understandable. Mark didn't want to come here any more than they wanted him."

"Your father wasn't the only one who resented the change. There's a lot of sympathy for him here and I'm sure you won't mind my saying this. Try to persuade him to come back, for he really belongs here."

"What about you, Ann?" she asked presently. "What will you do now?"

"I think I shall go to London," I told her, and I could see all the unasked questions in her face. "I think I should be able to find myself a job there all right, for the meantime at any rate."

She looked at me without speaking for a while, then she reached out and took my hand in hers. "I hope things will come out all right, my dear. I hope you'll both find happiness before long. Your father will miss you when you go."

"Yes. I'm glad that Jenny is staying in the

village."

When I went back into the study, Mark was not there and the letters were still on the desk. There was nothing for him to do there now in any case and I began to wonder if I should see him again. There was nothing for me to do either except clear out his papers, and I thought it better to leave that until after he'd gone.

I sat on the window seat, idly looking out, and I prayed that he would come. I didn't believe that this was the end of everything between us, but I was unhappy at the thought of not seeing him again before he left the island.

After a long while I heard his footsteps coming down the hall and suddenly I felt absurdly happy. I saw his eyes go round the room as he came in and then he saw me in the window seat and he came across to me.

He pushed the letters to one side and perched himself on the desk and sat looking at me, and I could see the change in him. Of all the moods and expressions I had seen in his face in the last few days only the sadness was left.

"I shall be leaving here later this afternoon," he said. "What will you do when I'm gone, Ann?"

"I shall get another job," I said, "just as I'd intended to."

"In Tollie?"

"No. I think I'll go to London."

He didn't try to hide his feelings from me this time, and his eyes shone as he looked at me. "In spite of all I've said, you still intend to stick around me?"

"Perhaps *because* of something you said. Something about an inevitable pattern, wasn't it? Our love is as inevitable as anything else in your life. You'll come to know that in time. I love you, Mark. I always will. I'll be there in London when you want me. But you'll have to come and tell me so. And you will."

Suddenly he was off the desk and pulling me from the window seat into his arms. For a long while he held me tight against him as if he would never let me go. Then just as suddenly he let me go and walked swiftly from the room.

I knew that was the last I would see of him on the island.

Chapter Nineteen

WHEN I arrived home that evening I told my father that Mark would be gone from the island before the end of the day. I also told him what Mrs Willis had said about Mr Martin wanting him back.

"Then there's nothing to take you across there again," he said.

"I'll be going back tomorrow to clear up one or two things, but that's all."

He looked at me for a moment or two, then he said, "Well, if I'm going back there's no sense in hanging around. I'll go over with you in the morning."

I was relieved to hear him say that and I saw Jenny's face light up too.

As we walked down to the boat the next morning he seemed quite his old self, striding out so that I had to hurry to keep up with him. Only a tiredness about his eyes and the sharpness of the lines in his face that were clear in the morning light showed the strain of the last few days. Yet there was a sadness about him too and I guessed that he felt more than he showed.

We walked in silence for a while, each lost in our own thoughts. Presently he gave a small sigh. "So I'll be crossing on my own again tomorrow. First Jenny, now you."

"All the same, I'm glad you're going back, Father. You know you wouldn't really be happy doing anything else."

As we came down to the jetty Tom looked in astonishment at my father. "Nice to see you back again, Mr Carroll," he said, and there was genuine warmth in his voice.

My father rested his hand for a moment on Tom's shoulder. "Thanks, Tom," he said, "it's nice to be back." There was friendliness in his voice and in his manner. It was the first time he had spoken to Tom since asking about the baby, for Tom had stopped coming to the house since I had come home. I knew now that he had accepted Tom and had decided to let the past bury the past.

The men shook hands with my father or patted him on the back, saying they were glad he was better, and I was happy to see him among them again. Even so, the journey across to the island was rather a silent one, and I guessed that the reason for the constraint was *my* presence in the boat rather than my father's. It must be common knowledge now how the accident came about and I knew that the sympathies of the village were with my father rather than me over the quarrels that led up to it. This was just as well since he was staying and I was going and I bore them no grudge for it. If I had not been there they would all, no doubt, have been talking about the changes over at the House and no doubt expressing their satisfaction that Mark was gone. In spite of their sympathy for him over Peter's death, I knew that they would never have come to like him. I had defaulted, gone over to the enemy camp, by showing my preference for him. Meg alone congratulated me on this. To her, Mark had always been "the Master", and always would be, and she could not get over the wonder of the fact that not only did I love him but he also loved me.

It was a relief, in a way, to know that Mark would be gone. Time would have to pass, I knew, before we could get back to where we had been and I felt that this would never happen so long as he stayed on the island. There was too much here to remind him of the past and at his best he had never been really happy here.

I went into the study to sort his papers ready to be sent on to him. That was all that was left for me to do now. Without him and without Peter the house was unbearably depressing and I would be glad to go myself.

On the desk I found a letter addressed to me in his handwriting. My fingers were trembling as I opened it. I don't know quite what I had expected, but as I skimmed rapidly through it tears of relief and happiness were running down my cheeks. I sat down in his chair and read it through again more slowly. It was really no more than a brief note.

"My dearest," it said. "As soon as I get to London I shall fix for you to stay with Bob and Barbara as I suggested to you once before. Even so, you cannot arrive alone and friendless in such a place. You have no idea how vast it is, enough to daunt even your spirit. Let me know how and when you are arriving and I'll be there to meet you and take you to them.

The last few days have been a nightmare. They made me a stranger to you. I shall never be able to thank you for standing by me and bringing me to my senses again. Without you I would have been lost. Without you I will be lost. I love you, my darling. I always will."

I read it through once again until I knew every word by heart. Then I folded it and put it in my pocket. I knew now that I could face anything.

It did not take long to sort out the papers and pack them up, and then there was nothing left to do, so I went along to see Mrs Willis.

"Mr Martin was asking if you were here," she told me. "I think there are one or two things he would like you to do before you go, but he's away out now and won't be back till after lunch."

I asked if there was anything I could do to help her and she said there wasn't. "It'll do you no harm to take it easy for a bit. Why don't you take a chair out into the sunshine."

"I think I'll just go for a walk," I said.

I went along the beach as I'd done so often before, knowing that it was probably the last time I would be walking around the island. When I reached the gates of the burial ground I hesitated and then on an impulse went inside. I had not been in there since Peter was buried and now I walked over to his grave. It was still covered with flowers. The sunlight filtering down through the trees gave me a feeling of remoteness as if I were far away from the sunlit world outside.

It seemed strange and sad to think that Mark would never stand here beside the grave, remembering Peter, as I did now. But remembrance is with us wherever we are and I knew that Peter would never be forgotten.

Some day Mark will have another son, *my* son, I thought, as if Peter would know my thoughts. In him you will live again for Mark. To him he'll give all the love he wanted to give to you.

As I stood there thinking of him it was impossible to believe that never again would I listen to his laughter, never hear his swift footsteps echo in the old house. He was still so much alive to me – his teasing face and the dark eyes which could be so serious as well as gay. Until that moment I hadn't fully realized how strong my own attachment to him had been.

Now the burial ground was a hateful place to me. Peaceful still and a fitting place for those who had lived out their lives. But not for Peter. He didn't belong here. He was too young, too alive. Oh, God, what a waste. Now I understood some of Mark's raving. Like him, I couldn't yet accept

Peter's death. It had been a mistake to come here. Swiftly I turned away and walked inland across the island in an effort to calm myself.

There was little for me to do that afternoon, and again and again I found myself brooding, going over and over things that had happened in the past. Small things, brought back vividly now just through being alone in those rooms. Strangely enough, it was Peter now, not Mark, who dominated my thoughts. I kept remembering what he'd said, where he'd sat or stood, how he'd looked. Perhaps it was because my worries about Mark and my family had been stilled, at least for the time being, and there was room now to let Peter in. Perhaps I had deliberately shut him out before, unwilling to face reality. Perhaps it was just being alone. Whatever it was, I found myself at last pacing the room, tormented by my thoughts. For a while I had a strange fancy that the House and the island were beginning to affect me as they seemed to Mark. I shook off the thought impatiently, but I was relieved when at last it was time to go down to the boat.

I was sorry to say goodbye to Mrs Willis. Her kindness and understanding had helped me all the way through, right from my first days on the island. So long as she stayed there, I would be in touch with her through my father.

As the boat drew away from the shore, I looked back, remembering my thoughts and feelings on the day I had first gone across to work there. How I had been so afraid of getting caught there, of being content to stay and grow old there and in the village, as everyone else seemed to be. Well, I was leaving it now, probably never to set foot on it again. For although I would come back to the village, there would be nothing to take me across to the island. I had the feeling that by the time I did get back, Mrs Willis too would be gone from the House.

Would it change much, I wondered. Would the village change too at last? Would the young people growing up, like Tom and Jenny, bring about the changes they'd wanted in their youth, or would they too grow staid with the years? Would Rob marry Meg and would their children be content to work on the island as they had been? Already they were idle questions to me, matters in which I would not be deeply concerned.

Jenny was out that evening, somewhere

with Tom. My father was tired after his first day back at work and went to bed early. I too was exhausted with all the varying emotions I had been through and very soon I went upstairs to my bedroom.

It was still warm and the sunset was beautiful across the loch. I opened the window wide and sat beside it. The familiar scene spread before me. The loch, the island and the hills beyond. I should miss them when I was in London, for they were part of me. As I looked at them, fixing them in my memory, I found myself in tears. I made no effort to stop them, and resting my head on my arms I let them flow unchecked. I cried for all that I would be leaving behind. My mother and the days that were gone; my father and Jenny, and Peter. Today I couldn't help but cry.

Tomorrow I would wipe away the tears.

Tomorrow a new life lay ahead of me.

Hρ